These Harsh Streets

These Harsh Streets

Tory Wilson

Library of Congress Control Number:		2011910165
ISBN:	Hardcover	978-1-4628-5121-8
	Softcover	978-1-4628-5120-1
	Ebook	978-1-4568-9359-0

To order additional copies of this book, contact:
Xlibris Corporation
1-800-618-969
www.Xlibris.com.au
Orders@Xlibris.com.au
500814

Contents

Note vii

Chapter 1 1
Chapter 2 9
Chapter 3 14
Chapter 4 20
Chapter 5 25
Chapter 6 34
Chapter 7 48
Chapter 8 60
Chapter 9 74
Chapter 10 83
Chapter 11 95
Chapter 12 113
Chapter 13 122
Intermission.. 137
Chapter 14 141
Chapter 15 160
Chapter 16 169
Chapter 17 183
Chapter 18 192
Chapter 19 204
Chapter 20 217
Chapter 21 234
Chapter 22 250
Chapter 23 258
Chapter 24 263

Chapter 25 273
Chapter 26 278
Chapter 27 289
Chapter 28 297

NOTE . . .

Before we get started I need to apologise. Everything you are about to read may not make sense. It has probably not been worded right.

Until recently I thought Grammar was what the music stars win at those award nights.

I may use a big word from time to time but don't let that fool you. Every three months I can hire a book from our little library. The last book I hired was a dictionary. I thought, if I have something to say I'd better get some of it right.

I never was good at school. Guess that explains a lot.

For the Joy in my life . . .

CHAPTER 1

Childhood

When I was 9 years old two things happened that impacted on my life in a big way.

1. My family moved house.
2. My dad thought it was time for me to learn to be a man.

Dad . . .

That's what I was told to call him but I never saw the resemblance.

'Boy', he would say through his alcohol-soaked lips, 'it's time you become a man'.

The old man would shove me toward the corner in the back room of our below-modest, suburban house and tell me that the only way I was getting out of the room was by going through him.

At first I was so young and naive I thought he meant that he was a ghost and I could walk through him. I quickly found this to not be the case though.

One black eye, a swollen lip and a crushed spirit was what I ended up with the first time he let me out of that dark, lonely corner.

Mum never knew. And if she did she was too afraid of my dad to say anything. Dad told her that when we went in the back room it was for "Man's Business". She wasn't to enter no matter what noises came through the closed door.

I don't know if she ever tried to come and save me.

Dad was, what I now know to be, a Dole Bludger. For those not up with the lingo, a Dole Bludger is someone who doesn't work. They have no job and they don't actively look for one. They live off the fortnightly payment that comes from the Government. The common term for that payment is called the Dole. To Bludge is to not work. So a Dole Bludger is, essentially, someone who doesn't work and takes money from the Government. That was my Dad. And because he was always home he had plenty of time for our teaching lessons. There'd be a good two hours each afternoon for us to be alone before mum got home and he made great use of it. Thursday nights were the worst.

It wasn't long before I avoided that back room at all costs, which was hard because it was my bedroom.

I'd lie in bed at night and imagine myself squashed into the corner with my back pressed against a big poster of Wally Lewis—The King. My childhood hero. I'd cower and sook like a baby while my dad would stand there arms crossed, shoulders back and smelling of beer.

He looked so proud. Proud. How fucked up is that?! (Sorry, I'm trying to stop cussing but it's hard in this environment). Proud that he thought he was teaching me to become a man and look after myself. All he was teaching me was that I hated him and needed to get away as fast as I could.

But for now I was stuck there. He was my dad. My Teacher. My Warden.

Mum worked endlessly to give us a better life. She worked at the local Chemist in the section where they handed out prescribed Medicine. That would be both a blessing and curse later in life. As hard as she worked it was never enough. Dad would spend any spare money we had on the drink.

Of course it wasn't always this way. We did have some good times. I clearly remember the car trips Mum, Dad and I would go on. Whether it was to visit far away relatives or a trip to the local shops, they would always be fun. When I was growing up Dad had a station wagon. Even though there was a perfectly good back seat that I could have all to myself, I still found it best to lay down in the back part of the car every time. Being only small I could fit, no problem. As the years went on I had to start lying diagonal but it was still a nice fit. I'd generally have to share the space with luggage or shopping bags but I didn't mind. And why was it so much fun? Because Dad would play music, he'd play it loud and we'd all sing along. Mum included. We had our regular tapes (They were tapes back then) that would be played all the time. My favourite tape was a mix of radio hits. We'd sing along to the likes of John Lennon. Dr. Hook. Johnny O'Keefe. Cold Chisel. John Farnham. The Beatles. All that classic Rock and Roll. I'd lie on my back and look out the window, watching the powerlines go past. Counting the poles as they came and went whilst belting out hits of the past and present, I forgot about problems at least for the duration of the trip. I think, looking back, this is where my love for music grew. Or in the least the plant was seeded. They were good times that were few and far but they did happen.

But when times were bad it was hard to get away.

My only escape from my dad was when I would hide out at my best friend's house.

His name was Craig.

All though he lived around the corner, Craig was only two doors down. If I stood in my back yard I could see straight into his yard.

I'm not an artist but I'll draw you a diagram. Just so you can get an idea of what I'm talking about.

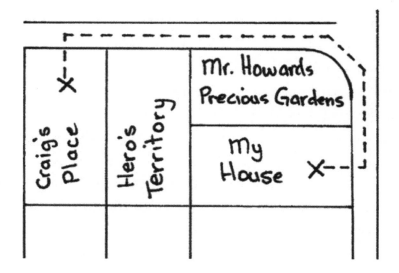

Two fences and a perfectly clipped lawn was all I had to cross to be in his yard. That and Hero. Hero was the big black dog that belonged to my neighbours.

I don't know what type of dog he was but I do know that he didn't like kids. Hero and I had plenty of battles. I'm proud to say that he never got a taste.

Hero was the sole reason for me having to take the longer trek around the corner.

57.

It took 57 steps for me to get from my front door to Craig's. I'd counted those steps thousands of times. I could've made the trip blind.

My dad did often.

I felt more at home when I was with Craig and his family. His mum accepted me, treated me like her own. I had a place set at their dinner table most nights.

And the meals! Oh my, the meals. Red meat! Vegetables! Pasta! Poultry!

At home my stomach had got use to a diet of Bread, Fish Fingers, Fish Finger sandwiches and the occasional takeaway.

Mainly Fish & Chips.

I'm surprised I never grew gills.

It was hard for mum to keep the fridge full of food when beer occupied most shelves.

I'm going to take this opportunity to get something clear. I'm not writing these things to get sympathy from you. If you feel sorry for me, please don't. I just want to tell my story. This is what I went through. Good or bad, it's my life.

Now where was I?

It never occurred to me to feel guilty for leaving my mum alone with that man every afternoon. But I had no choice. It was either that or the dark corner.

Which would you choose?

Most days I'd arrive home from school and would have to act like James Bond to get out of the house un-noticed.

Jump the fence to avoid the squeaky gate. Sneak down the side of the house and up the backstairs, through the back door which was always open. Tip toe into my room making sure to avoid the Wally Lewis poster. Dump my bag. Change my clothes and straight back out the same way.

Of course, sometimes I wasn't that lucky. If I came in at the wrong time I would catch dad going on a trip to the fridge. Or the bathroom. Then it was back to the bedroom but not to change clothes.

But when it did work I'd be in and out in two minutes flat.

Craig was always waiting for me on his front porch. I often wondered how long he waited for me on the days my Bond impersonation wasn't good enough.

We'd do a number of things to pass the time. What all 9 year old boys do; Cricket in the side yard. Marbles out the front. Pestering the neighbours. Tormenting Hero.

We'd never play in the backyard. From the bathroom window at my place you could see straight into Craig's backyard. Dad never cared where I was if I was out of sight. The minute he saw me I was summoned home for another lesson.

Sitting at my place around the dinner table with Craig and his family was where I loved to be. I felt like a king. I didn't even know the name of most of the food I was eating. But it was good.

By now mum had got home but was too busy dealing with Dad to realise I was missing. I never held that against her. I'd be the last thing on my mind too if I had a man like my dad overlooking me.

After dinner we'd take up residence in Craig's room to watch some TV. I'd get the signal from Craig's Mum that it was time for me to go home by her poking her head in the room and whispering two simple words.

'Good Night'.

57 steps and I was home.

Dad was generally in a beer-induced slumber by now so I could make it to my bed comfortably. No Bond moves required. Mum would generally greet me with a smile I knew was taking all her might to show.

Some nights I didn't hear dad's snoring and mum didn't meet me at the door. Instead, their bedroom door was closed and there was a constant banging of wood on the wall. Surely there couldn't be that many pictures to hang?

See. Naive.

This was how my life went.

And the worst part was I wasn't getting any better at my lessons.

CHAPTER 2
. . . .
Schooldays

I hated school and it never gave me a chance.

That's probably what you were expecting, right? Going by what I've told you so far. But you'd be wrong there. I loved School I just wasn't that good at it. As much as I tried, and I really did, I just couldn't get good marks. You know the feeling when you like something heaps and you try and try to be good at it but it's just not you? Well that was how it was with me and school.

When my family moved I had to change Schools. That didn't help none 'cause it's always hard being the new kid.

I went to the Local School. It was tough. You had to hang with the right crowd or know how to defend yourself. Even at my age.

I was a boy with no self esteem so finding new friends was almost impossible. I didn't know how to act in front of them. I didn't know what to say or do.

Craig went to a different school so I was forced to attach myself to any gang that would give me the time of day.

But there were two things at school that made my life a little bit more bearable.

1. Mr. Carter.

Mr. C.

He was my teacher when I was in Grade four. Our relationship didn't exactly start well.

On my first day at my new school I was sitting in class feeling like I had to get out. I put my hand up and Mr. C looked my way.

'What is it?' he said.

'I need to go to the toilet please'.

Mr. C allowed me to go to the toilet. I walked out of the classroom, down the end of the building and ran straight for the front gate of the school. That was my big plan of escape; ask to go to the toilet than run. I shoot out of the front gate quicker than a bullet from a gun. That's pretty quick.

It never occurred to me to run straight for home. I went the opposite way. I found myself running down the big hill towards my grandma's place. I ran straight in her yard, made for the laundry and bundled myself behind the washing machine.

I don't remember how long it took before my mum came walking through the door. She seemed to know exactly where I'd be.

Picking me up and carrying me to her car, she said one thing . . .

'Better not tell your Father'.

She took me back to school before returning to the Chemist.

Mr. C couldn't have been nicer about our first day together. 'Let's start over', was all he said as I took my seat.

I liked Mr. C.

From that day on I never asked to go the toilet during class. And if I did I always came back.

And my days of keeping the washing machine company were over.

2.   Sport.

More specifically, football

I was befriended by a crowd of boys that were part of the School Football team. They spent their lunch times sitting around talking about games from the previous weekend. I knew Football but I rarely got a chance to watch it. Dad always had some video of old TV movies playing.

That's where Chris' dad came in handy. He would buy the local paper every Sunday. I would study the sports pages every Monday and get all the information I needed to be able to involve myself with the lunch time talks.

Every Friday afternoon our team would visit a local School to play their Football team. We were pretty good.

We went through the year undefeated. I did my share. I never stood out as a player but I held mine.

My relationship with Mr. C grew and grew. He always asked me about my football and I always told him all about it.

But some days not even Mr. C was reason enough for me to get out of bed and go to School.

So . . . I devised a method for getting out of school on some days. Mum was so busy in the mornings getting herself ready for work and Dad was always hung over and snoring which meant that I could get away with not going to school and they wouldn't even know it. How did I do this you ask? I had one of those old single beds with the thin foam mattress on top of the wire base attached to the metal frame. The wire base was springy and would cave down with enough pressure. Since I so often used this set up as a trampoline my bed nearly touched the floor when I laid in it. And that's where the trick lay: All I had to do was make the bed, make it nice and tight, tuck the sides in so that it looked flat and I would then slide in under the covers and be lost within the drooping base. I'd pull the covers up over my head and keep still until I heard Mum's car leave. Then I'd be out of bed and outside onto the streets to pass the day.

That easy.

Mum often poked her head in my room but I guess she thought I had got myself up and ready and off to school so she left it at that.

I was finally found out and Mum wasn't impressed. Dad neither.

Extra lessons.

Anytime I got into trouble the punishment was always the same; extra lessons. You'd think I would've learnt.

And my parent's solution to this: dad ripped the wire base off my bed and replaced it with the door from the hallway. I went from having the most comfortable bed imaginable to sleeping on a door with a thin piece of foam in between it and me.

We can't always have it our way I guess.

CHAPTER 3

Girls—Part 1

Girls, girls, girls.

I know what you're thinking; a 9 year old discovering Girls. But it's true.

Well kind of.

During my 4th year at school I started noticing that the girls in my class were different than me and my friends.

We all noticed.

The girls noticed something very different. They came to the decision, seemingly telepathically (Webster's Dictionary, page 476) that boys were yuck and should be run away from.

It's funny though because Craig had a little sister. I never looked at her that way.

I asked my mum about girls one day.

'Mum, why are girls and boys different?'

I had caught Mum on one of the nights were she was standing in front of the stove.

'Why do you ask that?' was her response.

'I don't know. I see them at school and they're different'.

'Well of course they're different. Boys and Girls are different for the obvious reasons'.

It wasn't obvious to me.

That's when dad walked in.

'What, you don't know the difference between a boy and girl? Stupid boy'.

Mum bowed her head and kept quiet.

'Boy, we need to take you to a Brothel'.

He grabbed a fresh beer and walked out.

I had an all new question for mum.

'Mum, what's a Brothel?'

Mum shot an evil stare at the doorway where dad just walked. After, she turned to me 'Don't say that'.

I left Mum to cook and went to my room, still avoiding my classroom in the corner.

Now when I say I discovered girls, I mean one in particular.

Kim Reardon.

Kim was every boys dream. Long, blonde hair that was always put up in two pony tails. Beautiful smile. Skin more pink than the brightest fairy-floss. She always smelt lovely, like a rainy day. All the boys in my team knew I had a crush on her and they told here every chance they got. This embarrassed me so much.

She was in my class and was witness to my first day escape.

I did eventually live that down by the way.

Kim lived down the road from the school. Just about halfway between the school and my favourite washing machine.

My friends embarrassed me in front of Kim all the time. That's what friends are for, so they say.

I always wondered and still do now, who is the 'they' in that saying? No matter what the topic, 'they' always had something to say about it.

Strange?

I actually got the guts one day to say hello to Kim. No one else was around so when I told my friends they didn't believe me. Of course.

But it did happen.

She giggled and ran away. After a few steps she turned back, whilst still running, and said hi.

That's when I ran. The other way.

One day she was coming up some stairs and I was running down them. As we crossed I said, whilst trying to catch my breath 'Do you want to be my girlfriend?' I didn't even know what it meant but I asked her. To my surprise, and horror, she said yes. What was I expected to do now.

I told my friends and they didn't believe me, again. I told them to go and ask her. So they did.

Guess what . . . She said yes!

I was over the moon. It was my greatest day in grade four.

And then she kissed me and *that* became my greatest day.

How'd it happen? I was held down, that's how.

Pretty sad hey?! The first time I kissed a girl, Kim Reardon—the girl of my 9 year old dreams, and my friends had to hold me so I wouldn't run.

They caught me outside the library. Two friends I had at school came up and told me that Kim was heading my way. They had heard that she wanted to see what it was like to kiss a boy. And she was my girlfriend so she thought it may as well be me.

I was sitting on a bench reading through the book I had just loaned. My friends came rushing up and sat either side of me. One grabbed the book from my hands as the other took hold of my right arm. As the book was thrown to the ground my other arm was grabbed and I was pinned.

Then she came walking around the corner. Pony tails shining in the sun. Four of her little friends walking about 10 paces behind. Giggling.

I resisted against my captors but it didn't help.

Kim walked up to me, called my name and then leaned over.

When our lips met it wasn't front on. I was squirming too much for it to be perfect. But after the initial shock I was captivated. Her lips were soft. Marshmallows in Strawberry flavour.

My friends let go and I didn't move.

Kim's friends were standing back a bit. Hand over their mouth. Giggling in disbelief.

When our heads parted I nearly jumped in for seconds but she ran away. Her friends were in close pursuit.

My two buddies stood me up and patted me on the back.

No one remembered that I had to be held down. My friends told everyone how I was the only boy in 4th grade to kiss a girl. That wasn't his sister, mum or Grandma.

I was King for a Day. Fool for a lifetime.

CHAPTER 4

Home Life

Life at home never got better while I was in Primary School.

My days were spent at School and my evenings at Craig's, when I was lucky.

Mum worked the 9 to 5 shift at the Chemist.

Dad worked the fabric off the couch.

On the weekend I found it hard to find enough things to do that would keep me away all day.

I didn't want to be in my house. I hated it. It embarrassed me.

We lived in an old high level housing commission home. The house was on stilts and the underneath was all dirt. I must have used every inch of that dirt to make tracks for my cars.

Matchbox cars, I loved them!

Craig would come over and we'd build entire cities under the house. Race tracks. Hotels. Caves. It was best when it rained as the hotels got all posh ... pools.

I was ashamed of the house but I let Craig come over. He didn't care.

Our lawn was always big. Big as in high. Long. Dad never mowed it. Mum wouldn't know how and I was too small.

The clothes line was rarely used. Mum was either at work or running after Dad. She was always too busy to put a load on.

I could've helped there. I knew washing machines.

There wasn't a single sign of a garden—much to our neighbour's shame. Mr. Howard. Not the old Prime Minister. Our neighbour. He loved his gardens and the fact that our poor excuse for gardens bordered them pissed him off to no end.

Then there was the inside.

I don't think we ever owned anything new. Every item was either given to us by a family member feeling sorry for my Mum, brought from a second-hand shop or Dad brought the 'Gift' home. He always brought them home outside of shopping hours though so I didn't get it.

Mum never had friends over. I guess like me, she was ashamed.

It didn't stop Dad but.

We seemed to be hosting a different guy every night. And Dad seemed to know them all for different reasons.

'Freddie and I grew up together'.

'Bruce and I did time together'.

'Cook up something nice for Sammie. He's practically family'.

It didn't matter who it was. Dad treated them all the same.

Better than me and Mum.

Mum did her best to keep dad and his friends happy. As they sat at the table drinking booze, smoking cigarettes and talking shit, Mum would sit in the lounge room and wait for them to leave. She hated the thought of them leaving because that would mean all Dads attention would go to her.

I never understood that. She hated it when they showed up on the door step but she hated it more when they left.

The nights when more than one showed up were the worst. Dad would treat Mum like some trophy he won at the local pub raffle. Every few minutes he'd call her in to the kitchen and grab her right in front of his buddies.

Dad's friends would laugh and egg him on.

Mum knew if she didn't go in that she'd get in trouble. She didn't want that. Neither did I.

The morning after Mum would have to go to work with little or no sleep. Before she left she'd have to clean the mess left behind.

I don't think there was ever a time when the rubbish bin wasn't full, over-full, of beer cans or bottles before the day it was emptied.

Most bins get dumped into the big trucks with a thud and that was it. Our bin, when that was emptied, it sounded like someone pouring 1000 marbles into a glass jug.

Of course, there were times when life at home was good. Dad would be in a good mood which put mum at ease. Very temperamental (Webster's Dictionary page 476) was my Dad. Moody.

These were the times I actually enjoyed being with my Dad. We didn't have regular lessons in the corner. He would spend time with me doing stuff I wanted to do. Always in the house or yard but. We never went out. Except for the car trips I mentioned earlier. No park trips. No outings to the movies. Not once did we walk up to the local shop to play computer games. But we were at home and we were getting along and that was good enough for me. Even if, deep down, I knew it wouldn't last.

Sometimes he'd even hold down a job for a while. None of his wage ever went into the house though. Except the fridge. More specifically the beer shelf.

Dad went through hundreds of jobs. Every one of them he seemed to lose because of someone else.

'Damn fools! I was five minutes late from lunch. And they reckon I stunk of Beer. Bloody Joe, he was driving and got us back late. He insisted on visiting the drive-through on the way out of the Pub. If it wasn't for him . . .'

It was funny because every new job he got he seemed to be the boss.

'I start my new job tomorrow. I'm the supervisor so I can't be late. Yep, they hired me as Manager, I start Monday. They offered me a job as floor man but I told them no, I'm a Supervisor'.

He did have a lot of jobs but was still unemployed more often than not.

Craig's Mum would sometimes ask how Mum was going.

'How's your Mum doing Darling?'

'She's good' I'd reply, never convincingly.

Dad was never mentioned.

Craig's Dad didn't even ask me about him.

I thought guys knew guys. Not in our suburb I guess.

CHAPTER 5

Suburbia

We lived in a little suburb in the Western part of the Capital City in our state. The suburb was filled with mostly low-income families. Or lower. My family was no different. The suburb was beautiful but for the most part it was poor. The one thing it was rich in was characters. Man, there were some lively people.

The other thing it was rich in was family values. And I don't just mean your own. If you were born and bred in my Suburb you were all family. All you had to say was 'Man, I was born and raised in **Suburb omitted**' and someone had your back no matter what the situation.

My suburb was, and still is, the kind that people either love or fear. There's no in between. If you're out at a party or something and people ask you where you're from, as soon as you say **Suburb omitted** they will react in one of two ways:

1. They will make up a lame excuse to get out of your company as soon as humanly possible.

2. They will reply with something along the lines of 'Shit, my cousin lives there. Up the road from Kev Hooper Park'. Or 'Man, I'm from there. Born and Bred', and you'd have a new friend for life.

You see, the suburb never leaves you. I will always be proud of where I come from. I'm never embarrassed to say it and every chance I get I will do my best to promote it.

Later in life I had many occasions where I'd have to defend my beloved hometown. I'd be at a new job, sitting in the lunch room and the topic of bad neighbourhoods would come up. Well, since my hometown was only two suburbs away from where I worked at the time, **Suburb omitted** would always be top of the list. I had a defence speech memorised 'Man, I lived in **Suburb omitted** for the first 20 years of my life and I never had a problem. I'd walk down the street alone at 2 o'clock in the morning and feel as safe as you could possibly feel.

The person's response would always be 'Yeah but . . . Someone told me . . . I heard that . . .'. You see, they always tell you about stories that they had 'heard'. Shit people blab to them.

I have this to say; If you aren't from there and don't know what it's like, keep your mouth shut'.

I love that suburb and will always be grateful to it for giving me a feeling of belonging.

I made quite a few friends in that suburb. They all lived around the corner, in the same street as Craig.

Half a dozen of us formed the nucleus (Webster's dictionary page 333) of a gang. Well as much as a bunch of 9 year olds could be referred to as one.

There was me. If we were in a movie I would've been the quiet, unsure one. Always sitting back. Never leading, but if I didn't like what was happening I'd leave.

I did know what I wanted to do but I was never really fussed to mention it. I'd generally just go along with what was happening.

I knew wrong but. Back then. If someone suggested something that I thought was wrong I'd say I had chores to do at home. For the most part.

I was a part of the gang but I knew the rules.

Craig was next. He was the happy one. Always smiling and ready for fun. Wherever there was a good time to be had, he was there.

Sometimes he had too much fun.

We had a friend called Dallas. He was what you'd call the games geek. His day consisted of three things: playing games at the local shop, talking about the high scores that he beat every day & devising his dream job; making computer games.

Dallas was a good kid but had his priorities all messed. He'd miss a day of school every two weeks because he got caught up playing games at the shops.

He swore he'd died and gone to heaven the day the Atari came out.

His hero was Pac Man.

David was the rebel. Every gang has one. Most gangs are full of them. Well they'd like to think so. We had just one.

But he was enough of a rebel to make up for all of us.

If anyone had an idea that sounded half daring, Adam was all for it.

He wasn't always on the right side of the law. Shoplifting was a favourite of his. We didn't mind but. I mean who doesn't like free chocolate?!

He was so much of a rebel that he even had no spare time for girls.

Andy didn't have the same problem though. He was the ladies man.

His favourite saying was 'Where's there's girls, there's Andy'.

He had a new girlfriend every week. One week Sue. Gina next. Sam after that.

I think he had something to do with just about every girl in our block. And the dads knew him because of it.

Andy walked around our area as if he owned the streets. It actually got a little annoying. At least I thought so.

There was one thing he always said to me that made sense later in life. He'd say 'You know, if only you had a sister'.

I didn't get it back when I was young.

The last main fixture in our motley crew was Shane.

Shane was weird. That's really the only way to describe him.

Nowadays they have a term for him—Emo. (I hate that bloody word!).

Back than though the term would've been less flattering—Serial Killer.

Come to think of it I don't know which I'd rather not be called.

He was a freak. Always dressed in black. Listened to weird music. Viking-chanting type shit. Talking about death all the time. He studied killers for a hobby. Who does that?

People were scared of him. Not us but.

I think that's why our little litter never got picked on. One, Dallas may have been a computer geek but you wouldn't know it to look at him. He was huge for his age. But the main reason was because everyone knew that they'd have Dallas to deal with.

Dallas was crazy but he was good to have on your side.

Everyone went to different schools

We don't even know if Shane went to school.

And that was our gang. We were an unusual collective but it worked. There was always something happening that we wanted to be part of. We spent every weekend together. Whenever we could hang out after school we would too.

Neighbourhood barbeques and parties were a blast. All our parents would be there. There were always more ladies from the neighbourhood than there were men. A few of the guys only had their mums around nowadays. Their Dads had long since moved on to their next, younger broad.

And of course Dad was there doing all he could to attract the most attention. He would get a group gathered around him and spin the biggest yarns about his greatest adventures that never happened.

The other guys would take it all in as if it were the 6 O'clock sports report. They'd even try topping it.

To me it sounded like a bunch of men standing around comparing the size of their dicks.

'My dick's the biggest'.

'Yeah, well I have the widest girth'.

'Well, well—I've screwed the most chicks'.

Pathetic!

While this was happening, the ladies, and a few of the disinterested guys would sit around and talk about anything that anyone cared to bring up.

'My daughter's first recital is this weekend'.

'I got the greatest deal on a new kettle the other day'.

'Did you see that report on the today show about a new way to turn rubbish into soap?'

And we were somewhere in the middle. We were too ashamed to talk about our cocks yet and none of us had kid's stories to bore everyone with. Occasionally we would wander to either side of the yard to hear fragments of someone's tall yarn.

Even more rarely we'd find the eye of a local kid's female cousin that was dragged along by their over-excited and under-protective aunt and uncle. That's where you'd find Andy. Bless his soul. He tried so hard back then.

Dallas would be talking everyone's ear of about how he was going to make games when he's older. Craig was off making people laugh with his jokes and antics. David was trying to steal all the beers from the eskies.

And I was there simply observing.

Shane always disappeared most of the night. He'd show up at the end always complaining about something that's happened.

More often than not the parties would end one of three ways:

1. A massive fight over something that no one could even remember. For weeks after, the neighbourhood would be on knife's edge. Everywhere you walked you had darting eyes burning a hole in your front (They didn't try and hide the evil stares behind your back. You had to be thankful for that). As you passed each person you had to remember if you were on the same side or not. Sometimes their looks didn't make it clear cut.

2. A quite end. These endings were good. The drunken men, and some chicks, fell over and slept where they landed. Or they stumbled home on the shoulder of their next door neighbour. It wasn't uncommon to hear that Mr-so-and-so ended up in the same bed as Miss-what's-her-name? You led the other home and they thought it easier to lead each other to the same bed than get one home safe and have to go it alone from there.

     Or maybe it was just the booze.

3. And my favourite. The party would end with a huge sing-a-long. Everyone would be off their rocker, showing their age as they belted out the number one hits of the 80's. But I guess since it was the early 90's they weren't that old.

This, combined with the trips in the back of the station wagon, is where my love of music stemmed. More precisely—Rock and Roll.

But I think I'll leave that for later.

At the parties that ended in a we-are-the-world type situation there were no separate chat groups. The entire congregation (Webster's dictionary page 118) took up a spot around the fire that was burning away in a 44 gallon drum in the middle of the yard.

There were those few that thought they should've been the next big thing in pop in the 80's. A lot of the girls seemed to be channelling Madonna. The guys all thought they were David Lee Roth or Bon Jovi.

These voices could be heard over the top of all the others.

But us, me and the boys, we would be off taking this opportunity to raid the eskies. As the oldies belted out We Are the Champions, we would be down the dark corner guzzling as many beers as we could carry.

I think I had my first hangover when I was 9.

There was a time just after my 10th birthday when there was a party like this weekly.

That's right about the time I started putting up more of a challenge to my dad's lessons in the corner.

My rebellious years were officially underway. Teenage Rebellion had come early.

And meeting Scotty didn't help.

CHAPTER 6
. . . .
Pre-Teen Rebellion

Why is our species—The Human Race—compelled to be attracted towards troublesome or Recalcitrant (Webster's Dictionary page 396) people?

People like Scotty.

Scotty moved in as my neighbour just after I turned 10. I was in grade 5.

He seemed to have the perfect family. His mum was beautiful. She had long black hair that always looked like silk. She should've done those ads where the company is selling shampoo and stuff. I'm telling you. Wow!

His dad looked a lot older than her but they didn't seem to mind. He was given a kiss every morning as he walked out the door and an even bigger one when he came home from a day's work.

They were the perfect family. What a family should look and act like. In my books anyway.

How I envied them. Fuckers!!

And Scotty never appreciated how good he had it.

The first day I met him we passed each other up at the local shop—The Night Light. He bumped into me, turned around scolding and had these encouraging words 'Watch where you're bloody going dickhead!'

I was a timid, little 10 year old kid. This scared the hell out of me. My dad's lessons in the corner were doing absolutely nothing to boost my confidence. He persisted though.

You can understand my delight when I noticed this grunt of a kid walking into the house next to mine.

This was the time my mum came up with the most superb idea she ever had.

(That was sarcasm In case you were wondering.)

'Why don't you go play with that new boy next door?' she said to me one afternoon.

I looked at her with a blank expression.

'But I have friends to play with'.

On this particular day my Dad was drinking heavily, which is no surprise, and had a right awful temper, which I guess is also no surprise. Mum knew that if I stayed home I was in store for a lesson. The tell-tale signs were becoming more obvious and Mum's radar was never wrong.

I still argued though.

'I don't need a new friend. And I hate him Mum!'

'You don't even know him. When have you spoke to him? And besides, Craig is away with his family and your other friends could be god knows where! Go say hello.'

I huffed and puffed, even stomped my feet, but still I ended up jumping the fence that divided my yard from Scotty's.

I started on the bottom step and made sure I took all the time in the world to reach the door.

I knocked quietly hoping no one would hear. I looked over at my house and saw Mum poking her head through the curtain at the kitchen window. She had a come-on-you-can-do-better-than-that expression on her face.

I knocked just a bit harder and Mum nodded her head in approval.

Footsteps approached the door and the moment it opened I suddenly had good feelings about my decision.

Ah, Scotty's Mum. She stood there in a long summer dress, huge smile and even bigger warmth.

Voice of an angel.

'Well hello there little man'.

Man, she called me a man. The only time I was called a man was when it was on the end of a sentence like 'You're dead!'

'You're from next door aren't you?'

I nodded.

For some reason I had turned temporarily mute. I later learnt that all the good girls have that effect on boys.

'How can I help you?'

I had to word this right so it didn't sound like I was ordered to be there.

'My ... We ... I was told ...'

Thankfully, Scotty's Mum took control. Her eyes lit up as if she had a sudden realisation.

'You know, I have a son your age. He'd love to play with you'.

She turned her head back inside the house.

'Scott', even her shouts sounded angelic, 'Scott can you come here please'.

Scott's Mum gave me her trademark smile and guided me into the lounge room.

'Being new here, Scott hasn't got any friends'.

I don't think it's because he's new to the neighbourhood but how are you meant to tell a young kids Mum that their only son, the light of their life, is a rebellious, rude, disrespectful little shit?

I walked into a room that I thought only a King could afford. The TV was huge. The couch was made of leather—though I didn't know what it was at the time. There were family portraits on every wall and I tell you if you rubbed out Scotty and his Dad the photos could've been on the cover of the next girlie magazine.

I didn't want to ruin the couch but Scott's Mum insisted I sit down.

'Scott, come in here sweety'.

I had barely got my bum on the cushion when Scotty walked into the room.

I know there's a saying 'If looks could kill' but I tell you, I was expecting to be engulfed by fire at any minute.

'Yes?' was the first thing he said to his Mum but his eyes were on me.

And would you believe it, she sat down next to me and clutched at my shoulders.

'Scott, this is our new neighbour. He wanted to play with you. Why don't you take him out to the backyard and have a kick around?'

The smile was fake but his Mum didn't notice.

'Sure Mum, he looked my way, let's go outside'.

Scott's Mum let my shoulders slump and jumped from the couch.

'There you go. Have fun boys'.

And with that I was left alone with him. The terror child that nearly made me wet my pants with one comment at the local shop.

As we walked out the front door, down the steps and around the house to the backyard, I saw the curtains in the kitchen window of my house shuffle again. I could imagine Mum behind those curtains with a big, victorious grin.

The backyard was huge. Bright green grass and lovely gardens. What a contrast to my backyard. The most distinguishing feature of that being the hollowed out car shell and old washing machine crammed into the boot. Rust had long since covered them both.

'Your yard looks like shit!' was Scotty's opening statement.

I had only one response.

'Yeah'.

'Why's your yard so dirty?'

I had no answer to that.

I tried to change the subject.

'My name's . . .'

'I don't care'.

Gee, did this kid know how to make friends! But as much as I hated Scotty at that one moment I couldn't help but feel thankful to my mother. All she was doing was trying to get another activity that can keep me away from my home. More specifically, keep me away from my dad.

Scotty picked up a football that was lying in the corner of the yard. It looked as if it was brand new, freshly removed from the pack. I'm sure it never got used. Maybe his Dad worked too much to have time to kick a ball with his son.

Funny. Two extremes. Scotty's Dad was never around but he seemed like the best Dad in the world when he was. And my Dad was always around and, well, you can work out the rest.

Scotty booted the ball straight at my head, it seemed. 'Why are you here?'

It was a simple enough question so I tried to keep the answer the same.

'My Mum told me to come'.

I kicked the ball back to him. With no force.

'You kick like shit! Do you do everything your Mum tells you to do?'

'Sure, don't you?'

The next line from Scotty's mouth was straight from a dirty Western Film.

'Fuck that! She's not the boss of me'.

I was stunned. Not because of the language but because I thought 'how could anyone speak poorly about such a perfect creature?' My next thought was to dodge the leather missile bearing down on me. I didn't think quickly enough.

As I hit the ground Scotty came and stood over me.

'My Mum's a cow and my Dad's no better'.

I rubbed my head and stood up. 'She seems nice enough'.

'Well she's not. And how would you know?!'

Scotty picked the ball up from the ground and booted it over the back neighbour's yard. 'I hate Football!'

'Not me', I stupidly protested, 'I love it!'

Scotty snickered. 'I bet you get to watch it with your Dad all the time because he always seems to be home. My Dad, he's always at work but that's ok. I get to do my own thing than. Mum can't control me so she leaves me alone'.

I watched the ball bounce over the fence two yards away. 'No, my Dad doesn't watch it. At least, not with me'.

All of a sudden I wanted this conversation to end.

But it didn't.

'Does he work, your dad? Or is he a Bum? I see him at home all the time'

Damn my considerate Mum for exposing me to this talk.

I gave Scotty the line that I had learnt to spit out with total innocence. 'My dad is currently between jobs'.

'Bullshit! He's a bum loser'.

With this I lost my cool and rushed Scotty. He was way too quick as he stepped to the side and met my head with a sharp left hook.

I went barrelling to the ground with tears coming from my already swollen right eye.

Scotty stood over me with a grin beaming from ear to ear. 'You may be a dumb son of a loser bum but you're game. I'll give you that. I'll see you tomorrow'.

And with that he went back into his house.

I was left lying on the ground, sobbing and confused. What had just happened? Did I make a new friend by trying to attack him and letting him sock me one?

The bigger question was, and I never did come up with an answer for this one, why did I try to stick up for my Dad? Why would I care what anyone, especially Scotty, thought about my loser bum Dad?

Loser Bum? Shit, Scotty was right.

My parent's reaction to the new face paint I was wearing was totally in contrast to each other.

Mum reacted how any Mum would—She cuddled me so tight I thought my other eye was going to turn black. She ran a keen eye over every inch of my body expecting to find stab wounds and bullet holes. Eventually she released me from her loving grasp, ruffled the hair on my head and told me that maybe I should stay away from Scotty.

My Dad's reaction was a lot simpler—'Well', he said, 'looks like we have to increase your lessons'.

This was around the time I started getting better with his teachings.

It was also the time I started spending all my spare time with Scotty.

I still don't know why.

We saw each other the next day just like Scotty said we would. He asked me to walk to the shop with him.

'Stay away from him love', my Mum's words skated through my head as I started on the short walk to the shop.

Why didn't I listen?

My Mum's advice was justified the moment we walked past the Store Clerk and made our way down the lolly aisle.

'So, you pocket all the gum you can and I'll grab the chocolate.'

My eyes opened wider than a deer in approaching headlights.

'What? You want me to steal?'

'Well I don't have any money. Do you?'

My Mum spent every cent she made putting food on the table and beer in my Dad's gut. Of course I didn't have any money.

'No', I whimpered, 'I don't'.

Scotty was already stuffing chocolate bars into his deep pockets. 'Then what are you waiting for? Go on, grab some. And make sure you get Jelly Beans, I like them'.

As I stood there contemplating my next move I had all different kinds of scenarios flash before me. If I get caught my Mum will be embarrassed and my Dad, well this'd probably mean double lessons for a while. If I don't do it Scotty will think I'm a chicken, or still a kid. Hell, I'm 10 years old. I am still a kid!

Worse of all, if I do this it may lead to a life of stealing, gambling, drinking. I'd turn into my Dad.

But I was young and naive. There's that word again. Webster's Dictionary has its meaning as:

na·ive

[nah-**eev**]

–*adjective*
1.   having or showing unaffected simplicity of nature or absence of artificiality; unsophisticated; ingenuous.
2.   having or showing a lack of experience, judgment, or information; credulous: *She's so naive she believes everything she reads. He has a very naive attitude toward politics.*
3.   having or marked by a simple, unaffectedly direct style reflecting little or no formal training or technique: *valuable naive 19th-century American portrait paintings.*
4.   not having previously been the subject of a scientific experiment, as an animal.

Now that I think of it though, the situation with my Dad's lessons falls under the fourth description. All though, I *had* been the subject

But who was the animal? Guess that makes me it.

I started stuffing lolly bags into my pockets.

I must have stood there forever with these thoughts darting through my mind because all of a sudden I was alone in the aisle.

I heard Scotty shouting 'Hurry up, come on!'

I looked up at one of those large, circle mirrors that they have at the end of the aisles in most small, family-owned stores and saw the evil look on the face of the store owner perched behind the counter.

I grabbed my pockets and ran as fast as I could. By the time I got to the exit, the store clerk was obstructing my path. I saw Scotty run up behind him and kick the man right behind his knee. The clerk went down and I took this opportunity to run right past him, out the door.

Scotty was laughing as we ran. I didn't know what to do. I was scared shitless but, I'll admit, there was also an element of fun to it.

'That was hilarious! You should've seen your face when you thought he had caught you. Oh man, let's do it again'.

I was panting as I ran at full speed, several paces ahead of Scotty. 'Are you serious? We'll never be able to go there ever again'.

We had reached my yard when our pace finally fizzled out.

'Who cares? Fuck that chink!' Scotty was always so elegant.

I'd have to remember to ask Mum something when I see her next; 'Mum, what's a chink?'

We got through our whole cache in 2 days.

As you'd expect, our escapades got more daring. I actually started coming up with great ideas for trouble myself.

It was funny, when I was around Andy, Shane or even David I was never anything but a great kid. Sure I got into trouble like any kid does but it was different when I was with Scotty. My persona would change depending who I was with.

It wasn't long before I found myself in trouble. And, surprise, surprise, guess who I was with?!

But I'm thankful because if it didn't happen I never would've met 'her'.

CHAPTER 7

Grace

It was the summer break before my first year in high school. The weather was standard for this time of year; hot. That's it. One type of weather over the Christmas break—Hot!

(You may have noticed that I just mentioned Christmas in passing. It's meant to be the best time of the year for a 12 year old kid right? That's normally the case. Not in my house though. Mum accepted all the extra shifts she could get just to have enough money to place at least something under the tree for me. We always had a great tree but. And Dad took advantage of the festive season. I think he thought festive meant drunk. He steps up the alcohol intake over this period. Oh, the joy.)

Anyway . . . I've digressed (Webster Dictionary Page 121)

Most of the gang had gone away for the holidays. Dallas, Andy and Shane were home but I didn't see them much. If I have to be honest I don't think they liked Scotty and I know they didn't like me hanging around him. The sad part of this is, because they didn't hang around it gave me more reason to be with Scotty.

But on one particularly steaming hot afternoon I met Grace. And like the song, she was Amazing.

She was 79 years old and is the 'her' I mentioned at the end of the last topic.

Scotty and I were down at the local shopping centre. Doing nothing much. Causing trouble. Stupid stuff. The usual.

After two years of hanging around Scotty I guess you could say that I wasn't such a nice young boy anymore. I mean I was generally still ok but I definitely became a different person around him. He just had that effect on me. God knows why?

Scotty would urge me on any chance he got:

'Hey, go and steal the milk from that crate behind the store. I dare you to run into that store, push all the stuff off the shelf and run back out. $10 says you won't put this brick through that cars window'. He had a dare for everywhere we went.

And me, I'd do all of them. I wouldn't even hesitate although I did on this day. And I'm glad I finally went through with it.

We were walking past the bus stop at the back of the shops when Scotty spotted some easy prey. He gave me that look that I knew the meaning of all too well. He could say it without opening his mouth 'I have a dare for you'.

'What is it?' I said with resignation.

Scotty walked over and wrapped his arm across my shoulder, pointing at a particular bench.

'Go over there and snatch that ladies handbag'.

I looked to where he was pointing and saw the object of his latest ruse.

She was sitting down with a walking stick by her side that was leaning against the chair. There was a big brown bag sat on her lap. Her purple hair was scruffy but in a neat way. At her feet there were several bags that looked to contain Christmas decorations. She was the only person occupying the seat and had no idea what was about to hit her.

Or maybe I had no Idea.

I whispered in protest 'Her?'

Scotty jabbed my gut in a playful way 'What, you scared?'

He knew that line got me every time. I fought it this time.

My protest continued 'She must be like 100 years old!'

'So?'

'So, so . . . what If I hurt her?'

'Hurt her? All you're doing is snatching the bag from her lap. It'll be easy'. He knew he had me.

'I don't know Scotty'.

'She's an old biddy. They always have heaps of money in their purse. Just run past that way', he pointed at the other side of the bench, 'and grab her bag as you pass the seat. Then run over this way where I'll be and well get out of here'.

I caved. 'Fine, I'll do it. But whatever's in her bag, I get more'.

Scotty looked at me with what I think was pride. 'Ah, you're finally learning. No problem'.

I took a deep breath and slowly made my way around the bus station until I wasn't far from the lady on the bench.

Scotty hid behind a tall tree and watched from afar. I think, on that day, I was the brave one.

I know now that what I did was everything but brave. It was stupid, reckless and criminal. But it also introduced me to Grace.

I hid behind a nearby bus terminal waiting for my moment. When it came I ran straight for the seat and my waiting prey. No thoughts came to me as I neared the seat. I just ran.

And then the bus came. I even remember the number: Route 531. For some reason it made me change course. My direction was no longer targeted at the little old lady sitting peacefully on the seat, waiting for the bus that will take her to the safety of her own home.

I ran straight to the tree that Scotty was sheltered by.

'What the fuck are you doing? Why didn't you do it?'

I was panting, keeled over behind the tree. 'The bus scared me'.

Scotty and I watched as the 531 stopped at the terminal where the lady was waiting. It took off after a few people exited.

'Now look, she's gone'.

I looked over at the seat. The bus was leaving but the little lady hadn't got on it.

'Shit!' was my first thought.

'Great, she's still there. Go do it now', was Scotty's. The difference being that he voiced his.

I looked up and saw the prey rummaging through her purse. When she clipped it closed Scotty urged me to make my move.

'Go, now!'

'Okay'. I half shouted and made off for my starting point.

Again.

Scotty placed the tree between him and the foul action.

Again.

The coast was clear and I was on my way. I picked up speed real quick. I was a fast runner. A talent I misused?

I didn't have time to check for an approving grin from Scotty as I neared the seat. All it took was a second. A split second. And there was no looking back.

The little, old lady had no idea that her peaceful day buying Christmas decorations would turn out so bleak and terrible. Maybe, for her, it actually turned out ok.

I never asked.

Reaching down with one hand, I scooped up the handbag by its large handles and kept running. For a few steps anyway.

I could imagine Scotty's approving grin now. I don't know why I craved it. Acceptance I s'pose. Of any kind. But his expression would've changed in an instant.

I was a mere foot away from the chair, bag in hand, when it all came crashing to a halt. Literally.

I didn't see the step up on the path. My toes caught it and down I went. I landed hard on my stomach with the bag caught under me. People had started to notice what was happening and a few were making their way towards me. And it wasn't to help me up.

The little old lady bunched up the plastic bags at her feet, picked them up and at the same time took the walking cane in her other hand. She slowly got to her feet and hobbled over to me.

There was a crowd around me by then keeping me from leaving. Public justice. I caught a glimpse of Scotty through the many bodies in front of me. I don't know if he knew whether to laugh or scream in terror. He did a bit of both and then bolted. Talk about every man for themselves.

One man had caught me under the armpit.

Another lady was waving a finger at me telling me how I should be sorry and how some time in jail would do me good. Several people were talking amongst themselves discussing how my home life must be.

And then it happened.

I met Grace.

She walked over, made her way through the gathered spectators/justice keepers, whatever you want to call them and stood in front of me.

'Maam, do you want us to call the Police?' One guy spoke up.

'Of course she does' said a fellow spectator.

By this time one of the Shopping Centre Security Guards had heard the commotion and entered the ring of people.

'What's going on here?'

One of the gathering answered 'This boy just stole that ladies handbag and he tried to run off'.

My heart sunk. I was done in. I knew it. I still had the bag in my hand. I couldn't deny it.

The Security Guard grabbed me by my free arm and went to cart me away.

That was when she spoke up. Her voice was frail and polite. You know how it sounded. Just like your Nana's, I imagine. The nice one.

'Excuse me Officer. There has been some kind of misunderstanding. I know this young boy. He was bringing me my handbag. I dropped it and I'm far too old to bend down to pick it up'.

I was stunned. So was the crowd around us that had seen the whole event play out.

'What?! That's ludicrous', was the reply from a big burly man, 'this punk stole your bag!'

A little lady entered the debate 'And now you're sticking up for him?'

The Security Guard looked at me. All I could do was stare at my feet and ooze of guilt.

Grace reached for her bag 'Thank you very much Matthew. You're a lovely lad'.

She grabbed my arm and weakly pulled me away from the guard.

I was caught in a game of tug-o-war between a Security Guard that should be hauling my away by my hair and a little old lady who should be kicking me as I'm dragged along. Instead she was trying to free me of my guilt.

The Security Guard held on until the last possible minute. When he let go I jerked toward the lady—my victim. My saviour.

The Guard walked away with a shake of his head and the crowd dispersed. There were several small conversations going on between strangers. Hey, I brought the community together, even if for a moment. Even if it was in hate against me.

I was stunned to find myself walking back to the seat with the little lady. To this day I still don't know why I didn't just run the first chance I had. I'm sure glad I didn't though.

I helped her lower herself onto the seat. And before I knew it I was sitting beside her. We chatted as we waited for her bus.

'My name isn't Matthew Miss. And I'm awfully sorry'.

Grace patted my knee.

'I know love'.

'Which one?'

'Both. And I'm not a Miss dear. I'm an old lady. All old ladies are Mrs'. That's why you have grandparents and not grandparent'.

'So why isn't your husband here with you? Helping you? Protecting you from boys like me?'

'Oh dear, I don't need protection'.

She said the next part with a cheeky grin 'Besides, who would be cruel enough to do anything to a little old lady?'

Me I guess.

I pleaded my guilt and embarrassment again 'I am really sorry Mrs'.

'That's ok love. Mr passed away a little while ago'.

Geez, not only did I try to steal from a defenceless old lady but I did it to one who recently lost her life partner.

I was feeling the lowest form of scum at that point. But as a bus pulled up and the lady made to stand up I felt all the more worse. She reached into her bag, pulled out her little purse and handed me a crisp $20 note. Grace grabbed my hand and tried to place the note in my open palm.

'Take this love. Go buy yourself something'.

I lowered my hand and looked at the ground.

'No, I can't take this'.

Grace lifted my hand again, placed the note in it and closed my fingers around it.

'Please love, take it. There's better ways to get money'.

I now felt like the lowest kind of low.

As all of the plastic bags were bunched up and the walking cane was reached, grace made her way to the bus.

'Thank you Mrs' was all I could say.

I walked behind the little lady as she entered the bus. She seemed like a pro at it. By the time she was on the top step of the bus and at the driver she had the exact change ready.

The driver even greeted her 'Well good afternoon Grace. How was your trip?'

Grace looked back at me as she handed over her money to the driver 'Just fine thank you Driver, just fine'.

And then, the doors closed and she was gone.

I started my shameful walk home. As I walked I said one word . . .

'Grace'.

That was a Thursday. Pension day.

I don't know what compelled me but I was sitting at the same bus stop the next week when the same little old lady came to sit with me. She had a nice, friendly smile.

'Hello love'.

'Hello Grace'.

We sat and chatted for 15 minutes until the bus pulled up.

Graced didn't have a chance to bundle up her bags. They were in my hands and I was helping her up.

'Well, aren't you helpful?'

I didn't reply as we heading for the bus.

This time when Grace got on the bus, I followed her. The driver noticed this.

'Oh, hello Grace. I see you have a helper today'.

Grace patted my arm 'Yes, I'm a lucky old lady'.

We paid our fare, took up our seats at the front of the bus and chatted all the way to Grace's stop.

This same thing happened every week for a very long time.

I wasn't called "dear" or "love" for much longer. I told Grace my name after the third week. The bus driver even started greeting me by it.

I had found a friend for life.

So did Grace.

CHAPTER 8

High School

I may have loved Primary School but my thoughts towards High School were immensely different.

In the years preceding High School I hung around the guys less and Scotty more. This wasn't good. I never took advantage of High School like I should've. I know that now.

If I could give one piece of advice to anyone in this world it would be to stay at school. Try your hardest. You only get one shot at it as a kid.

It only gets more difficult after.

How different would my life be if, as a teenager, I could've concentrated from 9am until the home bell rang at 3pm? I mean, it's only six hours for Christ's sake!

Hindsight ... It's true what's said about that. But try telling that to a 13 year old.

You know, you were there once. Right . . .

Primary School was done and dusted before I even noticed. I had my favourite teacher from grade 4. You know, the washing machine saga, Mr. C, again in grade 7. He was my last full time teacher. Seemed like a fitting end.

I was a totally different kid the second time round though.

Scotty had certainly rubbed off on me in a big way.

And the results were painfully clear.

I wasn't the same shy, reclusive kid that Mr. C had taught 3 years earlier.

In grade 7 I was more and more becoming rude, vulgar you could say, and rapidly getting worse.

Moving into high school didn't help.

Especially since I had to share my home room with Scotty.

Out of all my friends from the local area, Scotty was the only one that attended the same school as me.

Most of the other guys attended the same school. Craig, Dallas, Andy and Shane went to a rather posh school four suburbs away. I envied those guys. Even more so when we hit High School.

David and Shane, when they did go to school . . . well, who cares?

Where was I . . . ?

Scotty and I ran a mock in our home class. We caused two teachers to request transfers. We sent a small, stocky lady to the hospital. Really, we were out of control.

I still don't know why I acted so differently around him. When I was with the other guys, at their house, going out with them, I was a near angel.

I *was* an angel according to grace but maybe she was biased.

Scotty just had that effect.

I think it was because, all my life—pre-Scotty, I was never accepted. I was a bit of a loner. I found it hard to make friends. I couldn't approach people and start a conversation. Still can't. Scotty made that part easy. At first he didn't even want to know me let alone speak. And when we did speak, he started it. All I had to do was nod my head and follow.

I will give Scotty credit for that but; he brought me out of my shell.

But as quickly as I was making friends through Scotty, I was chalking up twice as many enemies.

With my new attitude came a temper.

If anyone looked at me and Scotty wrong we would be on them. All talk but. Never fists. I fired up over nothing, thinking I was protecting some kind of honour we had. Any little niggle would tip me over the edge.

My change was really scary. It happened so fast.

One day a nice innocent. The next . . . trouble!

Luckily I found a legal outlet.

I found myself back on the field, just like I did in Primary School.

Football.

Rugby League for all the Europeans.

Rugby League allowed me to be as rough as I wanted. Hurt as many people as I wanted. And they put it under the same category; sportsmanship.

I'd found my calling. So I thought.

For 80 minutes I was a machine.

Now bear in mind I was never the biggest guy (60kg at my heaviest). But what I lacked in size I made up for with enthusiasm. I'd tackle anyone. A lot of them ran through me or over me but I got right back up ready for the next guy.

In fact, Football, sorry, Rugby League was actually helping me lower me aggression. Strangely enough.

Maybe because it took me away from Scotty. He didn't want to play.

'I'm not touching another bloke, he stated. 'And what about those scrums? You have your head between two guy's arses'.

I didn't care. Even when he teased me about it.

'What are you, gay?'

By this time I had learnt about all those words. I certainly wasn't gay. I'd even kissed more than one girl. One day I got to touch a boob. Under the bra.

More than Scotty had done.

I found something I enjoyed in Rugby League. I wasn't all that good but I liked it.

And that's what Grace had told me time and again.

'Boy', she would whisper (she always referred to me as 'Boy'. I liked it), 'find something you like. Something you enjoy. You don't even have to be good at it. If you enjoy it, do it'.

So I did.

We'd play every Friday afternoon. That was the beauty of it. Not only was it the greatest sport you could play but it also got you out of class every Friday.

Scotty didn't think this was much of a perk as he'd, more often than not, be wagging on a Friday anyway.

We had two teams in my year: A grade and B grade.

The A grade team was where all the best players were. These guys were future stars. Every one of them. That team filled up real quick. And I wasn't in it.

I made the B grade squad. There were a few in my team that nearly made the top squad but due to numbers they missed out.

A Rugby League team has 13 players on the field and 4 reserves. Times that by two teams and I was one of the best 34 players in my year. That's how I looked at it.

Grace too. She was so proud of me the day I went over her place to announce the good news.

She even brought me my first pair of football boots to congratulate me. It killed me to take a present worth $50 off a lady who lived through her means on a measly Seniors Pension.

The Government has a lot to answer for.

Sorry, I told myself, when I decided to write this, that I wouldn't get all political.

'Don't try to argue about something you know absolutely nothing about', was my Mum's advice. And I'm going to stick to that advice. I may not like what the Government does. I may hate the stupid decisions they make. I may think they're a pack of mindless, self-centred monkeys but I can do no better.

So I'll leave it at that.

But surely someone can . . .

Sorry.

Ranting . . . I do that a lot.

Just ignore me.

So . . . The A grade team went through the whole year undefeated. No one could get near them.

When it came time for the regional's, where they pick players from each school to make up the best team in our area and send them away to play the best of other districts, they may as well have sent our A grade team. And they did except for a few.

They won of course.

My team—B grade had an up and down year. We won a few a lost a few. All in all we did ok.

Every week I tried to get Grace to come watch me play. Most of the time we played at a school nearby. She could catch a bus or take a taxi.

I understood though when she said every week that it's too far for a little old lady to travel.

Maybe it was selfish of me to expect her to go.

Anyway, she didn't see a game all year.

Both teams made it to the finals. The first round, the Quarter-Finals, were played a week apart. My team played first, we won 18-6.

One week later the A graders won 48-2.

The next round, the Semi-finals, was played on the following weekend. This time the A grader's played first. They had a tight one. The score was 8-6 to the other school at half time. The second half was scrappy but they pulled through. The final score was 14-8.

The A graders were through to the Final. If they win that, it's on to the Grand Final.

Then it was our turn to play the Semi. We had to put up with several one-sided calls. Heckling from the sides and a much bigger pack but we won. The score was 18-16.

So there it was. Both teams were through to the Final for their grade. We were one game away from playing the Grand Final.

The day came for our Finals. Both games were played at our school on the same day. We got half the day off that Friday.

My game was first. It was a tough one. Our opponents were a local school. We knew most of the players on the team. It was more like a game in the local park against buddies.

After 20 minutes we were down 16-6. But we were hanging in there.

The score was 20-14 at half time. We thought we were well in it.

Most of the A grade team was on the sideline watching.

They couldn't believe, neither could we, that we'd made it this far.

The captain of the A grade side gave us a pep talk at half time. He didn't even seem nervous about his game that they'd play straight after we finished.

We stormed out of the sheds for the second half and blitzed the other team.

Final score was 28-26. And we were in the Grand Final.

Now it was time for the A graders to do the same.

If only life turned out as scripted as that.

They lost.

At half time they were up 16-0

But in the second half they came out a different team. They were cocky, trying fancy shit that didn't work. They dropped the ball every second set.

We were stunned. Sitting on the side celebrating our victory, we could only watch in shock as our main guys blew the biggest game of their lives.

Final score: 26-24.

Their coach, our Phys Ed teacher, reckons they had their heads shoved up their arses and deserved to lose.

The sheds went from the joy and cheer of our win to the sombre darkness of their defeat.

But we had to move on.

Grand Final day was a week away.

And the best part; the game was being played at the home of Rugby League in this beautiful country: Lang Park.

That was the castle that Wally Lewis reined as King.

The coach of the A grade side convinced our coach, he was the Woodwork teacher, to put some of the A grade guys on the bench.

I saw this as cheating.

The worst part was that some of our guys, who'd been there every game, had to miss out.

Luckily, and surprisingly, I wasn't one of them.

I had my spot, though I would start on the bench.

I asked Grace again if she could come and watch me play.

'Because this is your big game', she started, 'I would be happy to go and watch your team play'.

I was so excited.

It didn't even occur to me to ask my Mum or Dad to come.

Mum had to work and Dad, well, he's at the pub most Fridays.

Game day came around so quickly.

I was allowed to take public transport to escort Grace. She was just as excited as I was.

I could tell the trip took its toll on Grace but she tried not to show it.

Finally she was on her seat in the stands and I was on the bench waiting to go into the game.

The game was tight. The tightest yet.

At the end of the first half we were down by 4.

I looked into the almost deserted stands many times to see Grace. She seemed to be keenly looking my way every time. I think she dozed off a few times.

Bless her.

Second half kicked off and I was still keeping my spot on the bench company.

For the next 25 minutes there was no change in the score.

But with 15 minutes to go we got over the line. The game was tied and with a kick to come we could be in the lead. Our Goal-kicker lined the ball up on its dirt mound. He walked back to prepare. From over the sideline he ran in and hit the ball. It looked like it was going to make it the whole time it was in the air.

It missed.

The curve at the last minute took it to the left of the pole.

15 minutes to go and it's all locked up. The game was being played at break-neck speed. Or so it looked like from where I was sitting.

I was starting to get nervous. Not for my team. I was wondering whether I'd even get to play.

10 minutes left and the scores are still tied. The coach's head is swinging. It looked as if he didn't know where to look: the field or at me.

Each time he looked over at me I half stood up.

'This is it', I thought.

I was wrong . . . every time.

2 minutes to go and I'm still on the bench. I'd given up hope. I had got up off the bench and was pacing around.

My frustration had hit boiling point.

1 minute to go and the other team scored.

What happened . . . our star player dropped the ball, a guy from the other team picks it up and out-runs them all.

GAME OVER.

We lose and I don't even get a minute of play.

The mood in the dressing room was sombre, as you could imagine.

All the guys sat around with green-stained jerseys, grass filled boots and roughed-up knees.

Me, I was as clean as before the game. Not a mark on me.

I waited and waited for the Coach to have a chat to me. Explain why he didn't put me in. What was his strategy? But it didn't happen. He didn't even look at me.

That was it. I was out of there. I got changed, went and met Grace and we left.

The train ride home was quiet.

As always, I didn't start up the conversation.

'Well, I must have dozed off for some parts love but I think you played really well. I'm glad I come. Thank you inviting me dear'.

Her eyes must've been struggling to see the field, let alone the players.

I couldn't tell her that I didn't even get to play.

Could you?

For as long as I knew her, Grace talked about the day I got to play on Lang Park.

And just like that my first year in High School was over.

So was my Football career.

Yes, I called it Football.

Fuck It! The game sucks anyway.

CHAPTER 9

Lesson Learnt

If I do the maths I guess I was about 14 years old when I went into my second year of High School. I may have to work that out with a calculator though. I was terrible at Maths. It definitely wasn't my strong point.

Now, Art. That was what I loved to do. I looked forward to art almost as much as I longed for Rugby League. In fact, after the fiasco I just finished telling you about, art overtook Rugby League as my first love.

But I've finished rambling on about that so we'll move on.

The holiday break before my second year in high school was a heap of fun.

Scotty went away with his folks so I had plenty of time to hang out with the other guys. We met every day on the corner between my place and Craig's. Remember the diagram I put in near the start of this story? It took 57 steps to get from my door to Craig's. Yeah, that one. Well we met there.

We were all there. Me. Craig. David. Andy. Shane. Dallas. There were a few extra tag-a-longs that I didn't know that well but it didn't matter.

I was 14 (I have done the maths and I was right), hanging out with my best friends and not having a care in the world.

My Mum hated it when we sat around in the street. She would stand at the bedroom window that was on the side of the house facing the corner and scream out to us. 'Get off the street! Why don't you go down to Craig's? Stop throwing rocks! Come inside'.

She meant well, but you're not going to stop 6 teenage boys from doing what they want. Especially when they're in a group!

We were harmless. There was no trouble caused. We just hung out and talked.

These were my *good* friends remember.

Dad actually told Mum to mind her business and quit embarrassing me in front of my mates. (Just a quick note. That's the only time in this story that I'm going to use that word. I'm sure you know which one I mean. If not, too bad, I'm not saying it again. Don't get me wrong, I'm a green and gold-blooded Aussie but there's just something about that word. I don't like it. I promise it won't appear again).

Funny. One of the only times Dad actually supported me was when I was hanging around on the street like a bum.

It was one of those days, when I was out on the street corner until dark, that I went home and had my last lesson with Dad. Craig and I were the last two on the corner, which was the norm. We'd sit there for hours after everyone else had left and just talk about stuff. Anything. It didn't matter. On the rare occasion when there was nothing to say we would sit there and watch the cars drive past. I wish I could say that I remembered the day of the week it was, even the date, but I don't have a clue. Let's just say that it was the day that everything changed and nothing would ever be the same.

Mum was sitting in the lounge room watching TV when I walked in. Time unknown. She greeted me with her usual warm smile.

'Hello darling. You pair finally peeled yourselves away from that street?'

'Yes Mum', I would reply in a soft voice.

No matter how much of a pest I got when I was younger, or older, I always respected my Mother. You had to. For what reason; she was your Mum. Simple as that. She brought you into this world. For better or worse, you're here and you're alive because of her.

(Love you Mum XOXO)

'Well, your dinner's in the stove. Baked Beans, Sausages and Potatoes. It's still hot. Go and eat'.

I kissed her on the head on my way past. She seemed to blush and continued watching her program.

I don't think Mum had been kissed out of love in a long time. I made a note there and then to do it more often.

Not that I really cared, but I asked Mum as I started down the hallway 'Where's dad'.

Her reply should've made me run for the front door. Back door. Nearest window. Any exit I could get to.

'Your room, I think', she said with a quiver.

I was right outside my bedroom door by the time she had finished the sentence. That's where I heard the barking order.

'Come in here Boy!'

I had been in a good mood at this point. Hanging around with the guys always set me at ease. That mood quickly changed.

I could smell the alcohol before I saw him. Sitting on the edge of my bed with a beer in his hand, there was at least 10 empty bottles on the floor around him. Wally Lewis was giving me the evil eye in the looming, dark corner. The light was on in the room but that corner still seemed dark. You could shine a spotlight in that corner and it'd still look dark.

Maybe it was more the feeling of darkness than actual lack of light.

Either way, I was late for a lesson.

'Boy', he said as I dodged beer spittle, 'why do you hang around those jerks!' It wasn't a question, it was a statement. 'You should be with that kid next door. You could learn a thing or two off him'.

Having endorsement from my Dad to hang around Scotty should've been all the indication I needed that it was a bad idea.

I didn't answer him back.

The next four words he said were the ones I'd come to fear.

'In the corner boy'.

I almost pissed my pants every time he spat out that demand.

'Let's see if you've learnt anything yet. What are you, 12? You should know how to fight by now'.

"14", I thought but couldn't find the nerve to voice it.

'We've had hundreds of these lessons. You should be able to pass me. Now come on, I'm trying to teach you something. You have to be able to handle yourself out there'.

I whimpered into the corner, slammed my back against Wally Lewis and waited for the pestering. The first few slaps were light and on the cheeks. This was standard. They were to warm me up. Thanks Dad, real considerate. After that he let a few stronger blows hit my arms and chest. There would be constant verbal assaults to accompany the physical lesson.

'Hit back you girl. Put your guard up. Wait for an opening and hit me . . . If you can! Do you have the guts to hit your old man?!'

And that's when dad said the thing that made me snap.

'Come on, your Mum put up more of a fight when I taught her the same lesson.'

I mean I fucking lost it! And do you know what, I was proud. Of course, I knew Dad had hit her once or twice. There was always a bruised eye or swollen lip as indication the next morning. But to think that he shoved my Mum in a corner, probably as dark as mine, and told her to fight her way out. Now that was all I needed.

I made my charge.

Dad swung his left arm over my head and brought his right around to knock me on the back of my head. When his ribs were exposed on his left side, I ducked his right and landed a decent clenched right fist into them. This stunned him for a moment and gave me a chance to connect a left flush on his chin. He was down. I couldn't stop. As he lay on the floor and covered his head from my constant blows, I was swinging as fast and hard as I could. I'm sure less than a quarter of my attempts found their mark but I swung that many times that even that much would've amounted to a lot. At one stage he managed to grab my leg and pull me to the ground. I didn't stop when I fell I simply changed my weapons. I was on my back and kicked out with both feet. This is when I did the most damage which I'm sure wasn't Dad's intention when he pulled me down. His head was in perfect position for me to treat it like a football. It was like I was marching on thin air. Left, right. Bang, bang! Left, right. Bang! I broke skin and my shoes were being splashed with crimson-coloured justice. Eventually my Dad's defence gave in. He was helpless. I had stomped him unconscious. I didn't notice until I heard Mum's scream.

'Stop it! Stop! What're you doing?'

I couldn't believe it. After everything we had had to put up with from this man, she was worried about him. I was stunned. Even more so when I looked over to see the damage I had inflicted on my Dad.

I stood up and straightened up my clothes. I looked down at my bloody shoes. That scared me. I didn't think I was capable of such a thing. I guess you don't know til you're tested, hey?

Mum knelt down beside Dad and flicked the hair away from his face. There was blood all over. You could barely recognise him.

I was furious.

'Are you fucking happy'! Is this what you wanted? You want me to be a man, fine. How's that for you? Have I learnt my fucking lesson now *Dad*!'

And then I said the corniest thing I think I've ever heard anyone say.

'School's out Bitch!'

I started to walk away as Mum stood up and grabbed me by the shirt.

'My god! Don't you know I'll be the one who gets punished for this!?'

'I don't care Mum' (I did care but that hadn't even occurred to me). 'He deserved it. What did he expect?'

'I don't bloody know what he expected, but not this. Oh gee, what've you done?'

My temper was calming already as the realisation of my actions was setting in. 'I did what he wanted. I got out of his little cage. For the last 5 years he's done this to me, he had to think that one day I'd get past'.

'Not like this'.

'And where were you for all that time, hey? Why didn't you do anything?'

Mum didn't deserve that and I regret to this day saying it. I knew she was as scared of that man as anyone could get of anything.

I guess my temper was still a bit high.

That was the first and only time my Mum hit me. She looked at me with a face that I will never, ever forget. It haunts me almost every night. I'm sure there was a tear falling from her eye as her open hand struck my face.

As I ran out of the house I could hear Mum trying to wake Dad up. The last thing I heard before I went through the front door was Dad's voice.

'What happened?'

That was to be my last lesson. The next morning I woke up and, to my delight, and surprise, there were no new marks on my Mum. I was certain he was going to take it out on her. So was she.

I walked into the kitchen where she was sitting at the table having her morning coffee. She looked up at me and smiled. What else could you do in such a situation? I didn't dare ask where he was. Still in bed I was guessing.

I spent that day over at Craig's place. We listened to music (Which I will definitely get into later), played cards and just lazed about on the front verandah. As night time fell I headed home as Craig and his family were heading out for dinner. I contemplated wandering around the street for a few more hours to avoid having to go home but I decided to face the truth.

It wasn't what I expected.

As I walked in Mum was sitting on her favourite chair in the lounge room watching TV. She smiled and kept watching. I leant over and kissed her on the cheek. She patted my arm and told me to go and eat my dinner: Baked Beans, rissoles and potatoes. As I entered the kitchen Dad turned his head in my direction. He was sitting at the kitchen table eating his meal. There was no beer anywhere to be seen.

'Boy' was all he said before he looked down to his plate.

I didn't respond. I grabbed my plate from the stove, took it to my bedroom and let it go cold. That night I changed the furniture in my room around, took down the Wally Lewis poster and made a pact that I'd never let anyone get the better of me ever again.

Babies are a different story.

CHAPTER 10

Siblings

Life at home for the next two months was quiet. Mum spent her days at work and nights cooking dinner, cleaning dishes and watching TV. My Dad was a different man after that event. He looked at me differently, when he bothered to at all. He spoke to Mum like a human. Asked how her day was. Helped her with the dishes. He even took her out for dinner a few times.

Dad found a job just before I started my second year of high school. He worked as a labourer in one of those factories that build every little mechanical thing you could possibly need. Nuts, Bolts. Cranks. Nails. Screws. Hinges. You name it. It meant that every day when I came home from school, he wasn't there. Neither was Mum. Instead of having to sneak in and out of my house to avoid detection, then darting out the back door to go visit Craig, I got home, threw my bag on my bedroom floor and sat in front of the TV. In a nice, quiet house.

Mum and Dad genuinely seemed to be enjoying a purple patch. (Is that the right term for when things are going well for a certain period?) And I think it was my fault. Well all thanks to me anyway. I stood up to Dad. Showed him that he can't push around people all the time.

I should have done it a lot earlier.

Mum would beat Dad home from work most days. She would walk through the front door in her white Chemist coat, looking like a surgeon and start with the same three words 'Off my chair'.

I would chuckle and move, always with a smile present. Mum would sit in her chair whilst I moved to the three-seater and stretched myself out over it. We would sit there in a pleasant silence until Dad got home. He walked through the door, kissed Mum on the lips, said 'hey' to me and went to the kitchen. Mum looked at me and smiled. She was happy. The happiest I'd ever seen her. Even if it did come from a negative situation, the outcome was positive.

Life around the area was the same, besides the change at home. No one ever found out about my final lesson. It was none of their business.

When school started me and the guys went our separate ways during the week. I hung out with them less and Scotty more. We weren't in the same home class at school this time but that didn't prevent him from rubbing off on me even more.

I felt like I was living three separate lives. There was the quiet, easy-going me that showed him when I was around the guys. The on-alert, yet generally relaxed me that was present when I was at home and then the bad, getting worse, bullying me. That was the side Scotty brought out. We'd spent every lunch time together at school. It was just him and I. I always wondered why we never had more friends. It never occurred to me that I was the only one that could handle Scotty's presence.

Dad stopped encouraging me to hang around Scotty and Mum encouraged me to stay away from him. I thought about reminding her of the day she stood at the kitchen window and made me go over to his place. I didn't bring it up but. I was trying not to do anything to upset the peace that we were experiencing at home. I didn't know how long it'd last and when it did end I didn't want to be the cause.

It became real clear to me just how well Mum and Dad were doing one day when Dad came home from work. Mum hadn't gone to work that day. I heard her and dad talking the night before about the Doctor's appointment Mum had the following day. I didn't think much about it at the time. There could've been hundreds of reasons Mum had to go see the doctor. Not that I could think of many. But I'm sure there was. Of the few I thought of, none of them was close.

Mum was sitting in her bedroom on this particular afternoon. Dad walked through the front door, nodded his head towards me with the customary 'hey', noticed Mum wasn't on her chair in front of the TV and made straight for their bedroom. I caught a glimpse of Mum as Dad closed the door. She was sitting on the edge of their bed, crying.

My first thought was that something was wrong. Depending who you ask, maybe there was.

After a few minutes the bedroom door opened and my parents walked out. The puffiness and redness around Mums eyes told me she had shed more than a few tears. But there was also the tiniest hint of a grin. Dad looked slightly timid. I'd never seen him like this.

Mum sat beside me on the three-seater whilst Dad stood to the side. Mum signalled for Dad to turn the TV off. He did so.

'Darling, I have something to tell you'.

I didn't know what was coming but I knew I wasn't prepared.

'What is it Mum? Is everything ok?'

'It's fine dear'.

Dad couldn't stand still. His left foot kept tapping the leg of the couch as his right hand kept the beat on the backrest. Mum gave him a silent stare that said 'Stop that please'.

He stopped.

'Now I don't know how to tell you this so I'm just going to say it: I'm pregnant'.

I was stunned. Shocked.

Mum grabbed Dad's hand. She smiled at him.

'Really?' That's all I could say.

Dad spoke up 'Certainly is'.

I looked at Mum as she waited anxiously for my reaction.

'Well ... that's, that's great'

Wrong reaction!

I've learnt over the years that when a girl tells you she's pregnant, no matter who it is; a friend, your sister, a stranger, your cousin, your wife or girlfriend, your Mum, you have to react in the same, non-hesitant way.

'Oh that's fantastic! I'm so happy for you. You're going to be an excellent Mother'. And you have to say it as if you're the happiest person in the world.

So when I answered Mum with a stammering 'Well . . . that's, that's great' in a voice that lacked any enthusiasm, you can imagine that she didn't respond well.

She was silent.

Dad was even more so. He grabbed my Mums shoulders and hugged himself in to her.

I didn't know what was expected of me next. 'When are you having it?'

'The baby is not an *it*!' Mum softly but pointedly answered.

'I'm sorry Mum'.

'That's ok love. I am 12 weeks, so that makes the baby due in 6 months. It'll be a winter baby'.

Does it matter what season you're born in? Does it have some kind of effect on you later in life? Summer babies are more prone to illness? Autumn babies make for better doctors? Winter babies make great swimmers? I don't know if that's how it works. I'm a winter baby but I've never been to the Olympics to compete as a swimmer.

'You're going to be a big brother'. That was the most words Dad had said to me in the last two months since . . . since that night.

Shit. I hadn't thought of that. I'm going to be someone's brother. Big brother! What did this mean? Would I have to look after them all the time? Babysit whenever Mum and Dad weren't around? Keep them in the straight and narrow? (I was having enough trouble doing that with myself).

But what did my Dad mean by it? Did he expect me to teach my little brother or sister the same way he did with me: With his lessons? No fucking chance!

No, he didn't mean that. Surely?

That night we all sat around the table to eat dinner. We were acting like a normal family. Maybe the new addition will help us become closer when it arrives. Isn't that what they do? Married couples have babies just so they have a reason to stay together. That's what I hear. I wonder if that is why Mum let Dad knock her up?

The next 6 months flew by so quick that, before I knew, I was holding my new little Sister. Not up at the hospital. I never made it up there. I regret that still; not getting up to the hospital in time to see my new sister. That's the sort of thing they never let you forget either. As soon as she was old enough to talk it started 'You mustn't love me that much, you didn't even come up to the hospital when I was born. What do you care, you weren't there when Mum had me'.

Never let me forget. Bless her.

Mum spent one night and one day in hospital. She was out and home before I'd hardly had a chance to organise transport for myself. Dad was up there all the time. He didn't want to drive all the way home just to turn around and go all the way back.

Truth be told, Dad was slowly sliding back into his old habits. He'd sit around drinking all night and be too hung over to get up for work the next day. He lost about four jobs that way in the 9 months that Mum was pregnant. He'd have the occasional, slowly becoming more frequent, spat of abuse to hurl at her. And let me tell you, doing that to a heavily pregnant woman doesn't go down well. And he'd even started to give me a shove or two. Now that I'd graduated from his lessons and become a man, he'd want to test my new found manhood. I never bit back at him. I kept the peace for Mum's sake. And I still didn't think I could beat the old man in a full-on fight. I beat him once, once when he was absolutely sloshed. I put it down to a fluke. A lucky situation. I probably couldn't do it again. Although I was getting more and more chances to take him on again while he was drunk.

I never found out.

The day Mum came home from the hospital I had left school early to be there. As the car pulled up Dad tooted the horn. I ran out as quickly as I could. I was so keen to see this new baby. Find out who she looked like: Mum, Dad, Me? None of us? I guessed, as she is a girl she'd look like Mum. That's how it works. I think? Hang on . . . then why didn't I look like Dad?

When I saw her my heart leapt. She looked exactly like Mum. Spitting image. And that's a good thing. Beautiful. I know you think I'm weird. I mean how many guys say that their Mum is Beautiful? But it's true. In her younger days Mum was a knockout. Little Susie was no different. Even at one day old you could see the beauty. It shone for all to see.

Susie grew up so quick. Its funny how everyone else's life flies by so quickly and yours always seems to be lagging behind. Maybe that's because you're too busy watching the other lives that you forget to slow down, sit back and enjoy your own time. I know I did. And before you know it you're an old man sitting in a little room writing about the shit you missed out on.

What a waste!

For some reason, I tried at first to resist getting close to Susie. I don't know why. I don't know what it was that made me think 'This kid is not part of my family. I don't want to know her'. That didn't last.

I swear it must have taken all of three days before I found myself leaning over into her cot, singing songs to her in the morning. You know the song; 'Wake up, a little Susie, wake up'. She loved it. I always got a smile. Mum would walk in almost every day and catch me doing it. At first I tried to hide it, I denied doing it even though she had caught me red-handed. But after a few times I didn't care. Mum and I even did it as a duet occasionally.

I'd race home from school to see Susie. She was always asleep but I didn't care. That simply gave me more opportunities to sing the song to her.

I could tell Mum was enjoying the time with Susie. She loved being home. There was no way she was not going to be there to see all the firsts in her life—first smile, first burp, first real tear, first fart, first fall, first time rolling over, first time sleeping through, first time sitting up, first time crawling, first big bath, first solid meal, first solid nappy, first time using the potty, first step, first word.

Mum took Maternity Leave to make sure she was there for all those firsts. She was looking forward to staying home for a year to have, and bring up Susie.

Dad didn't take any kind of leave to help Mum . . . He just left!

I still remember it so clearly. You don't forget the day an Imposter walks out on you, your Mum and brand new sister. Brand new—she still had the hospital shine on her.

Two months into little Susie's beautiful life and Dad was heavy into the grog. The novelty of having Susie around wore off on Dad really quick. I don't think it ever hit him now that I think about it.

On the mornings where Mum and I would be leaning over Susie's cot singing to her, Dad would be snoring away, off key mind you, in bed.

If we woke him up he'd be grumpy for the rest of the day. Hell, he'd be grumpy anyway. Who am I trying to kid.

Now don't get me wrong. Dad was excited for the first few weeks. Not excited enough to make our duet a trio. But he did put some effort into it. He would take Susie out of her bed in the morning, when she was crying, and carry her around. He stopped the crying to give Mum a chance to sleep in. It was very thoughtful of him. That only lasted a week but. Before too long he was complaining about the terrible shrills coming from the cot. Mum would have to get up and take Susie into another room just to keep Dad happy.

This happened on the morning Dad left and never came back.

Susie was being more boisterous (Websters Dictionary page 45) than usual. It was made worse by the fact that Dad had downed a large amount of stubbies the night before. I know he did because the bottles were spread out over the kitchen table waiting to be cleaned up the morning after.

Mum took Susie into the back room, next to mine, and tried to calm her. It wasn't working and Dad was having none of it. Susie kept screaming for 15 minutes solid. Mum tried everything, including our duet. Didn't work. Dad got out of bed, stormed down to the back room and it was on.

'Keep that damn baby quiet! Can't you shut her up?! What the fuck's the matter with it?'

"It". He called Susie an *it*!

I should've punched him out there and then. Mum beat me to it. Holding Susie with one arm, she lashed out with the other and slapped him on the face.

Dad's reaction was quick but long lasting.

'Fuck, I don't need this. I'm out of here.'

And that was it. He was gone. The man I had called Dad for the last 14 years was out of my life. Out of *our* life.

That wasn't the half of it but. After a day and night of non-stop crying, Mum called me into her room. Susie was sleeping peacefully in her cot as Mum was sat on the edge of her bed.

'Sit down darling'.

I sat at the end of the bed, facing Mum.

'What's wrong Mum?'

She spoke softly. 'Now I know I don't have to tell you that your Dad and I didn't have the perfect relationship. That was quite clear'.

'I know Mum. What's this about?'

Mum lowered her head, pinched her nose with her thumb and index finger then spoke up. It was as if she thought for a quick second, got sick of thinking and putting it off, than blurted it out.

'He wasn't your real Dad'.

I was shocked. I was elated. I was confused.

'What?'

'He isn't your father. He came along when you were 8 months old'.

I asked the only question I could think to ask 'So who's my real Dad and where is he'.

'I'll tell you another day love. I'm too tired'.

I didn't want to push her.

'Ok Mum'.

I never pushed the topic. I knew one day, much later on, the subject would present itself.

This did answer one thing though . . . That's why I never looked like him. There was no Father/Son resemblance because we weren't Father/Son.

To prevent confusion, anytime I refer to him I'll call him Impostor Dad. That's if I mention him at all. We both know he wasn't my real Dad so it'll help keep the story simple. I hope.

I though having one person walk out of my life was bad enough.

I was not prepared for what happened after.

Then again, not many people are prepared to face death.

CHAPTER 11
......
Death—Part 1

I'll have to skip ahead a few years to tell you this part of my story. I assure you that you didn't miss anything. My life between the ages of 14 and 18 was pretty uneventful. Actually, that isn't entirely true.

If you give me a quick minute I will brush over an event that was certainly an eye-opener.

In my suburb we had a place where all the kids hung out. We all got together on a Friday night and caused trouble. Immature trouble, mind you. But there was one night it got very grown up. We had our little gangs I guess you'd call them. Just like any other teen hangout. And this hangout was the local Roller Skating Rink. Kids of this generation are probably asking their Mum or Dad; "What's a Skating Rink?" Trust me. They were big back in the day. Anywho, on this particular night, I was probably about 15 I guess, and I was there with a few friends and it was the end of the night. The Rink had closed and we were all standing out on the street just passing time. Talking shit and hitting on girls. We weren't having any luck with the girls so we took to talking shit. All of a sudden there was a whole heap of commotion within a crowd up people next to us. I heard screaming and shouting and then someone yelled out "He's bleeding!" This definitely caught our attention so we ran over to see what the fuss was about. Turned out that some guy had been stabbed. He was a guy that you wouldn't call a genuine local but he had been around for some time. Strangely enough, he had just got out of jail after doing a bit of time for assault. The irony. When we get to the crowded sidewalk we spot a guy sitting in the gutter with blood gushing from his stomach. He had been stabbed by some fella that didn't like the way his girl looked at this guy.

Fancy that—being stabbed because some chick looked at you wrong. Despite that I still always felt safe in my suburb. Sometimes things like that just happened and there was no avoiding them.

An Ambulance showed up minutes later and the victim was in the back geting tended to. He refused to go to the hospital so they worked on him in the van. Stitched him up right there. As I walked past the ambulance I overheard one of the Paramedics say—

"This'll happen on these harsh streets".

But back to my topic.

After my Dad left it took Mum a while to come to terms with it. She spent many days which stretched out to weeks moping around. Looking lost almost. I think if it wasn't for Susie and me, mainly Susie, she would've gone crazy.

Eventually Mum got over it. She stopped noticing that Dad wasn't around anymore. It's a strange thought that you could possibly miss someone that was nothing but bad news, but it happens. I can vouch for that. She missed him dearly for a while. It took her at least a year to be content with how her new life was. She did get there but.

I supported Mum any and every way I could. I'd offer to stay home from school every day to help with Susie (Mum never fell for that).

I started taking care of Susie so Mum could get away for a few hours. She would go around and have coffee with Craig's Mum. That's normally when Craig would come over to my place. We'd sit around, play video games and listen to music while Susie played on her rug on the lounge room floor.

As Susie got older Mum started going back to work. She'd work a few hours a week to start and eventually she was back full time.

Susie would go to the local day care centre whilst I was at school.

I wasn't at school for that long after Susie was born. I left, dropped out, before the end of grade 10. As soon as I turned 16 that was it. I was out. (Worst decision ever!).

I was right on Scotty's coat tail when he left. Not that I blame him. But . . .

I do have a quick, rather amusing (I think) story I want to tell you. It won't take much time, and then I'll get back to the other topic, you know, the Death.

In fact, I could blend them in. We'll see.

I would've been 16. As I said, I had left School, and was going nowhere. I had no direction.

What I did have was a girlfriend. She was a year younger than me and she was a little cutie. I won't go into detail or tell you her name because it doesn't matter.

I did spend over three years with her, and it was a great time, but I won't go into it.

Anyway, one day my Girlfriend was at my place. Mum was at work and Susie was at day care. We were playing around and it was getting pretty heated. Clothes were on the floor and beds were rocking. We weren't '*doing it*' yet but it was getting close.

And then she said the four words that every guy both feared and loves at the same time . . . 'Do you have protection?' Those words are feared because if you answer no, you ain't getting it. They're loved because if you answer yes, well hold on boys because you're about to get lucky.

Me. My answer was 'No'.

But I had a but. 'No, *but* I can get some'.

I was off the bed quick smart, pants around my ankles and dangly bit rock-solid and banging against my belly button. (Does that sound like I'm being big-headed saying my manhood was hitting my belly button? Well it was). I picked up my phone and dialled.

'Hello, Mayfair Pharmacy'.

'Mum, can you bring me home some condoms?'

'What?' was all she could say.

'Condoms Mum. Rubbers. I need some'.

My Mum was silent for a moment then whispered 'What size do you want?'

What size? I looked down at my stiffness. How was I meant to know? I'd never measured it. I had nothing to compare it to. Was it small? Big? Huge? Tiny? Regular. I went with the safe guess.

'Regular I guess'.

'No idiot, do you want a 12 or 24 pack?'

Talk about embarrassment.

'12 please'.

'Right darling. I'll bring them home today. Can you hold out until then?'

Smart Arse!

'Yes Mum', I whimpered, 'Thank you Mum'.

I guess she was just happy that I wanted protection.

I hung up the phone and went back to the room where my girlfriend was eagerly (that's what I want to believe) waiting for me.

'So?' she said.

'Mum's bringing some home. We can muck around a bit but'.

She hopped off the bed, fixed her clothes up and went out of the room.

'No, we'll wait. There's no rush'.

That night Mum came home, gave me the 12 pack and wished me luck.

In case you're wondering, that wasn't my first time. That happened just after my 16th birthday. It was some girl. Nothing great.

Funny hey? I thought so.

Well . . . it was while I was with this Girlfriend that Death visited.

I had turned 18 and was planning on celebrating with the guys. My birthday was during the week so a drink was planned for the weekend. Friday night we would go to the bottle shop and stock up. Saturday would be the get together. That was the plan. I shared a beer with Craig on my birthday. Our first legal drink together, the first of many we would say.

It never got past Friday night.

I was sitting at my Girlfriend's place, waiting to be picked up from the guys when the call came.

It was my Mum.

'Mum, why are you calling? Where's Craig, he's meant to come pick me up'.

The silence should've warned me that something terrible had happened.

'Mum?'

'It's Craig.'

Those two words shattered me. I didn't want to hear what came next.

'What, what's wrong?'

'There's been an accident love.'

'What happened?'

My girlfriend was in the background watching TV. She could only hear my side of the conversation but that was enough for her to turn the TV off and listen.

There was silence from Mum's end. She started sobbing.

'You'd better come on home love. Is there anyone there that can bring you?'

'But Craig is coming to get me. I'll be there soon.'

Mum's voice rose 'Just see if anyone there can bring you home. We'll talk when you get here.'

I covered the mouthpiece with my palm and spoke to my girlfriend.

'Do you think your brother can drive me home?'

She nodded 'Yeah. What's going on?'

I didn't answer.

'Yeah, Keith can bring me. Tell me what's wrong'.

After silence again Mum responded 'There's been an accident'.

'Yeah, you said that'. I was losing my cool.

'Craig has been in a car accident'.

My heart stopped. Literally.

'Is he ok?'

'He didn't make it'.

My legs gave way and buckled under me.

I was speechless. What are you meant to say? I looked at my Girlfriend with what must've been the worst expression she had ever seen. She knew. I didn't have to say anything.

'Ok Mum. I'm coming home'.

'Ok. I'll be here when you arrive'.

I hung the phone up and just stood there. Staring out into nowhere in particular, my chest seized up and tears fell down my cheeks.

'What's wrong?' my Girlfriend asked.

I couldn't answer. I walked straight down the hallway to ask her brother to take me home. She stopped me along the hall by grabbing my arm. I spun around to face her.

'Craig's dead'.

Her hands went up to her mouth and she was stuck to the spot.

I walked in to her brother's room, asked him for a lift home then went and waited by his car.

My Girlfriend didn't come with me. I had to do this alone.

You know what people say; 'You don't know what it's like to lose someone you love'. Well I do. I lost someone that was a brother to me. He wasn't *like* a brother, in my mind he *was* my brother.

I miss him so much and think about him a lot. (RIP Limpy).

When I got home my first reaction was to try and go over and see Craig's family. My Mum advised against it saying that they didn't want anyone there. I thought that didn't apply to me. I was family after all.

Mum asked me to respect their wish but. So I did.

I asked Mum to tell me what happened. I wish she hadn't.

Apparently the driver, some guy I didn't know (but will always hate) was being reckless, speeding over humps and swerving aimlessly. They were going along a road that had many, sporadic streets crossing it. These acted as intersections. At each section the road lumped. If you went fast enough you could get airborne. That was what he was trying to do. The passengers may have been egging him on. Craig included. I never found out.

After one too many humps, the driver lost control and swerved to the side, straight into a tree on the footpath. The tree, and street, was only 4 blocks from my place. They say you could hear the thump from Craig's place.

Imagine the eeriness that came with the realisation that the thump you heard moments ago was actually your son ploughing into a tree at high speed. Craig's Mum had that eeriness by the end of the night.

Craig was sitting in the back of the car. Middle seat. They had just left the bottle shop and were heading home before coming to get me. They were meant to pick me up before the bottle shop visit. I was meant to go with them.

To this day I think: 'I could've been in that car. I *should've* been in that car'.

As the car lost control and ran up the gutter Craig was taking a drink from his beer. The impact forced that beer bottle into his mouth and down his throat, where it shattered into a million pieces. Amongst the carnage he was slashed open from left shoulder down to the right of his stomach.

He died instantly.

Andy wasn't so lucky.

What Mum failed to tell me, maybe she didn't know, was that Andy had also been in the accident. He was in the passenger seat.

They ripped him out of the mangled car and took him straight to the hospital where he fought for his life for three days.

Eventually we got the call that he didn't make it. He was bleeding inside. I believe they call it Internal Haemorrhaging.

Just like that I had lost two of the best friends any person could ever want.

I couldn't sit still at home so I did the first thing that I could think of—I went to see Grace.

It was pushing on midnight but the thought of having to wake her didn't cross my mind. There's probably not too many people that you could knock on their door at midnight and they'd be happy to see you.

I tapped on the back door several times with no answer. I almost thought about turning around, walking down the front porch and heading home to sleep. I doubted that I'd get any though.

It took a few minutes but the door finally opened, very slightly. The chain was keeping any would-be intruders from entering.

'Who's there?' You could tell she was still half asleep.

'It's me?' I didn't have to say my name, she knew who it was.

'What's wrong dear?

The door closed just enough so that Grace could take the chain off. When it was pulled open she was standing in the doorway in her old-lady nightie (No disrespect).

I walked through the doorway and stood in the kitchen.

Grace closed the door behind me and walked over to the kitchen bench. 'How about I put the kettle on love?'

I didn't respond.

With the kettle boiling away, Grace took two mugs out of a cupboard and filled them with teabags and sugar. She got the milk out of the fridge and placed it next to the mugs.

There was silence whilst the kettle boiled.

Grace stood with her back to me, watching the kettle boil while I just stood there.

The whistle of the kettle didn't even break me out of my daze. I was a motionless ball of a wreck.

Grace walked over to the kitchen table with a hot mug in each hand. She hadn't noticed yet that I was still standing there. She placed both cups on the table and came to stand in front of me.

'Grace' was all I could muster.

Grace didn't need to be told what was wrong. Whatever it was, she knew it was bad enough to get me in this state.

She held her arms out and I took the offer. I embraced Grace like I had never hugged anyone ever. Not even my Mum.

And then I sobbed like a little bitch. I couldn't help it.

Grace held me for so long that I lost track of the time. I do know that when I had my first sip of the tea Grace placed on the table it was cold.

We sat down, Grace poured two fresh cups of coffee and I told her everything about that night.

I nearly told her about my Lessons but decided against it. I've never told anyone about that . . . until recently).

The only time I even came close to losing my cool was when Grace started with the God and Jesus garbage.

'This is God's will love. He has a plan for each and every one of us'.

What type of sick fuck would have a plan that involves my best friend being carved up with a beer bottle lodged down his throat as he slams into a tree at high speed?

I don't believe in God. There were times in my life that I thought I believed in him but that quickly faded, along with my reasoning (We'll get to that pretty soon). I just don't think one person, or being, or thing, or whatever you want to call him, created everything and everyone that you see in this world. And I sure as hell don't think that he has pre-planned everything that will ever happen.

Destiny. Fate. I don't believe it.

Most of the time I don't even know what I'm doing tomorrow. How can someone that I've never met know what I'm going to do every second of every day until the day he decides to off me?

Not possible.

God has a plan for all of us—Bullshit!

I believe in the Big Bang Theory. One day, billions of years ago, out of absolutely nothing, everything was made.

That's more likely than some guy creating it all isn't it?

I think so.

I got through her preaching without upsetting Grace.

By the end of our fourth cup of tea it must have been three am and Grace was setting up a pillow and blanket on her couch.

I settled down onto the couch and caught a few hours sleep. Craig was in my every thought. Andy too.

The next day I woke up and went home. Before I left Grace made me breakfast and we shared another cup of tea.

She said that I could go over any time to talk to her. I took her up on that offer so, so many times over the years.

I walked through the door and found Mum waiting for me. She wasn't mad at me for staying out without telling her, she was just waiting to tell me something.

'Honey, Craig's Mum wants to see you'.

I didn't need to have it repeated. I was out the door and round to Craig's in two minutes flat.

As you could imagine, the mood was dark. Craig's Mum was sitting at the table with family that had shacked up there to give support. His Dad was sitting on the back verandah nursing a beer and a few tears.

The walk from their gate to the front door was the longest 5 metres I'd ever walked. So many thoughts. So many.

I tapped on the door, slid it open and walked in.

Craig's Mum embraced me before I had a chance to close the door. I know it's a poor choice of words but she nearly squished the life out of me. I was trying to be strong. Her tears were flowing down my cheek. Eventually they had to fight with my tears for territory.

That day we sat around Craig's house and told stories about his wonderful, but far too short life. I had so many stories. We had been through so much together.

They say talking helps. I'd have to agree.

And then the Funeral came.

You only really ever find out how liked you are at your funeral. All through your life people may treat you like a friend. They act as if they like you but, then again, people are also good actors.

It's the people that turn up at you funeral that you can list as true friends.

Of course, like always, it's too late by the time you find this out.

I hope it's true what they say. You know, that you can watch your funeral from heaven (Gee I hope I'm going there. I don't hold out much hope). Then again, you have to believe in something in the first place before you can start hoping that it's real. Well, if it is, I'll be sitting there with pen and paper in hand writing up my haunting list. And who would be on it; every one that pretended to like me while I was alive but didn't care to attend my funeral.

I don't think Craig would've even needed a pen and paper from where he was watching. I reckon everyone he ever knew was there. I bet people that he had only ever passed once on the street was even there.

There were hundreds of people.

I never knew it at the time (I found out later and was pissed) but there was an open casket. They had cleaned Craig up and gave everybody one last look. I saw the casket at the front of the church but the lid was closed by the time arrived. Maybe it was for the better.

I like to remember him how he was.

Andy's funeral was a smaller affair. Not to say that he was any less liked. It may have just been that not as many people crossed paths with Andy in his time on this earth.

Do you want to know the hardest part of it all but?

The bastard that was driving the car that killed my friends went to Andy's funeral but he didn't make it to Craig's. I was furious. How could that ... the ... that Fucker go to the funeral of one man he killed but not the other?

Craig and Andy were missed terribly. Still are. But after a while I had to let it go and move on. Every year I have a drink on the anniversary of their death to celebrate their life.

I've drove along that road, past that tree many times since and it always gives me goose bumps. I'll never fear it though.

Now that it's later in my life, there are times, long periods of time where I can go without thinking about them at all. I feel guilty when this happens but i'm assured it's natural. You have to live your life right? (I'm not sure if that's a question or statement.

I'll always miss Andy and his ways but it doesn't compare to my life without Craig. We went through so much together growing up in a small suburb having nothing but friends and fun to pass the time.

I'm forever grateful to Craig for so many reasons. His death showed me that you never know when your time will be up so you have to live every day to the fullest. I probably went a little overboard with that.

I will tell you one thing; I can't listen to Van Halen's classic song 'Dreams' without thinking about Craig. It was his favourite song, from his favourite band.

I don't believe I'm going to quote Joan Jett but—'I love Rock N' Roll!'

CHAPTER 12

Rock N' Roll

I couldn't tell you about my life without devoting some page space to Rock and Roll.

Anyone that knows me knows that I could talk for days, weeks even, about Rock and Roll. I could give lessons on the subject. I wouldn't actually teach people how to play Rock n Roll on any particular instrument, I would teach, what could you call it? "Rock and Roll appreciation". I could be a professor of Rock.

I'm going to call this part of my story the self-indulgence bit. Please don't hold it against me.

I've been told by a few guys here that I should start a Blog. I don't even know what that is. But I will tell you this, if music is the language of the world than Rock and Roll would have to be its main dialect.

I mean, I really love all kinds of Rock and Roll. From all of the eras. What do we have? Let's list them:

50's—Buddy Holly. Richey Valens. The Big Bopper. (The Day the Music Died). Eddie Cochrane. Bill Haley and the Comets. Let's not forget The King himself—Elvis Presley. Chuck Berry. BB King. Johnny O'Keefe—Australia's own King of Rock and Roll.

60's—We'll start with the obvious—The Beatles. Some people say 'Where would Music be if the Beatles hadn't come along?' To those people, if they were here now, I'd say 'Please see the 50's list above'. Music was in pretty good hands already. I will admit though that The Beatles have probably had the biggest influence on music to date.

They did it all and, for a large part of it, were first to do so. How incredible is that middle bit of 'A day in the life' where the instruments are all building up to a climax and then release to a ditty, little beat—'Woke up, got out of bed . . .' Brilliant!

And you'd have to mention 'Sgt. Pepper's Lonely Hearts Club Band'. That whole album was, *is*, a classic.

Truth be told, you could fill a thousand books just discussing tracks from The Beatles. Lord knows plenty of people have.

Lennon and McCartney—Pure brilliance!

From the 60's we could also list—The Rolling Stones. The Beach Boys. The Easybeats. The Animals. Cream. Jimi Hendrix.

Jimi Hendrix is by far my favourite musician of all time. He is THE GREATEST GUITARIST OF ALL TIME. Anyone that disagrees, bring me your argument and I'll find ten ways Jimi bettered that. The way he worked that guitar, oh boy! If you've never seen any footage of him at Woodstock, do yourself a favour and go looking for it. Everyone raves about his rendition of The Star Spangled Banner but, for me, his version of "Red House" is what made that performance so memorable. Sheer brilliance! You can feel every note he hits. And the scary part—He breaks a string part way through and doesn't miss a beat.

And then you have the "Woodstock Improvisation". Years later you discover it wasn't all improvised. There were snippets of songs he was working on at the time of his far-too premature demise. 'Bollero' for example. His fingers move so quickly during that track you can barely keep up. And then, when you think he's pulled out all the tricks, he stretches his thumb backwards, *over* the top of the neck, four frets while his other fingers hold a chord. If you don't play guitar, let me tell you, that's not an easy thing to do. If you do play, try it. I dare you.

He was a freakin' genius.

70's—Wow, what a time the 1970's were. For starters, I was born. Then you get Balls-out Rock like—Led Zeppelin. Black Sabbath. Deep Purple. Chain. Kiss.

The bands of the 70's lived hard and fast but for the most part they didn't do it openly. I think. The flower power era was just finishing but people still believed in it. They wanted to see bands out making a difference. Living hard but living safe. Taking care of each other and appreciating the audience. Crowds didn't want to believe that bands were smoking every sort of narcotic possible, snorting even more and drinking their bodily mass worth of alcohol.

Led Zeppelin, to me, made the 70's. Jimmy Page in his prime was a sight to behold. When he pulled out that double-neck Les Paul you knew 'Stairway' was coming. Then all you had to do was sit back and enjoy just about the greatest composition ever written.

It was also an added bonus that they had the greatest Rhythm section there has ever been. John Bonham and John Paul Jones got grooves going that would have had Marvyn Gaye screaming for more.

Ozzy and Black Sabbath started the trend of writing the scariest lyrics you could imagine. And they backed it up with haunting music that buried itself into your soul and plucked at your intestine.

The track of their namesake is a prime example.

'What is this that stands before me . . .' The bell chiming in the background and crunching bar chords is sheer evil.

80's. It took me a while to appreciate the 80's era music but now it's one of my favourite. Where do we start? I'd have to say the Big Hair Bands ruled the 80's. They were pure, pedal to the metal Rock. No bullshit, just four guys playing instruments as loud as they could. You had Poison. Motley Crue. Van Halen. Skid Row. The boys in those bands lived fast and rocked hard. I think that famous Rock and Rock term was penned because of the big metal bands of the 80's—'Sex, Drugs and Rock n' Roll!' How those guys are still alive I'll never know. Like Nikki Sixx. The driving force and bass player for Motley Crue. I read his Autobiography. He was a mad bastard. Talk about living life on the edge. He was *over* it and somehow kept clinging on. How do you top that intro to 'Kickstart my heart?' You can't.

I will always love the hard-edge Rock from that era. Heavy Distortion, loud drums, sleazy lyrics and even sleazier women. What a life!

That, my friends, is why every young boy wants to grow up to be a Rock star.

And then we get to the 90's. Big Hair Bands pushed into the 90's. Guns N' Roses. Metallica. Ugly Kid Joe. Warrant. Mr. Big.

Guns n' Roses definitely picked up where Motley Crue left off (If they ever did). Axl and the guys were crazy boys. They lived by that famous moniker that, I think, the Crue invented. I must say, I don't think much of Axl Rose. I've read a few books on Guns n Roses too and he seemed like a bit of a Douche. Slash and Duff were the shit in that band! Those guys kicked-arse, let you recover then came back and kicked it twice as hard. I've read Slash's Autobiography and he seems to think rather little of Axl also. Guess that explains the band break up. I know Guns n' Roses are together, touring these days but, let's be real, that isn't *the* Guns n' Roses. It's just Axl with a back-up band.

You also had the new 90's type band—Pearl Jam. Nirvana. The Foo Fighters. Soundgarden. Rage Against The Machine. Alice In Chains.

Grunge. It was probably the natural next step in Rock after the Big Hair Band scene started to fade. How could you not love it but? Heavy Guitar. Cool as Fuck Riffs. Double-Kick drums. Lyrics that you could relate to. I was hooked.

And I have to tell you, I think Dave Grohl is the Ultimate Rock God. You know Dave Grohl. Everyone knows Dave Grohl. The drummer from Nirvana.

After Kurt Cobain's unfortunate death (I'm still convinced it was murder) he picked up a guitar and formed The Foo Fighters.

As big a fan as I was of Nirvana I'm glad they split up because, if they hadn't, we never would've been blessed with The Foo Fighters. And that would've been a crime. I dare you to disagree.

If you ran a poll and had people choose between Dave Grohl and Eddie Vedder for Rock God supremacy I don't have to tell you who'd win.

Do it.

Dave will win every time.

Oh yeah!!!

Rock and Roll is a funny thing. I don't remember the exact first time I heard it, in the back of the car I suppose, but I do remember that I have loved it ever since.

Craig and I spent many, many hours sitting around listening to Rock and Roll. All the classic 80's big hair bands and the 90's Rockers were our favourites. The groups I mentioned in the last two sections above dominated our tape deck.

I'm sorry that he never got to hear the bands of the naughties. You know—the two thousands. 21st Century. I think he would've loved it.

Bands like—Rise Against. The Mars Volta. Muse. The Living End. Each and every one of them has taken something from bands gone past, mixed it up and reinvented the wheel.

I think, If I were to be asked who was the most creative, musical genius of the current era I'd say it would be a challenge between Matthew Bellamy from Muse and Omar Rodriguez-Lopez from The Mars Volta.

Matthew writes the most amazing piano pieces, classical-type shit, and backs it up with out-of-this-world guitar. His voice is electric and, with his band Muse, they make the most incredible atmospheric-rock know to man.

Omar is a different kettle of fish all together. He plays the most intricate, off kilter guitar since Jimi Hendrix. But on top of his guitar playing, it's his compositions that are astounding. He directs The Mars Volta through so many time changes you forget which you are in. And they never miss a beat.

Their energy on stage is intense. There's no other word for it. I have never seen a band play with so much emotion. Their singer, Cedric has a lot to do with that. The guy is a hyped-up jackal. I think he channels Robert Plant as well.

Trust me I've seen them live four times. They are a sight to behold.

Matthew vs. Omar? I'd have to give it to Omar, only by a hair though.

If I had to throw in a third to round it out it would be the band Tool. Not any member in particular, the whole band. They are right up there with The Mars Volta for weird time signatures. None of this standard 4/4.

But I guess no one did ask me, so . . .

Look at The Living End. They are steeped in a form that was created 50+ years ago—Rockabilly.

Nobody is ever going to invent a new type of Rock and Roll—music for that matter, but there's nothing wrong with putting a twist on an old, tried and tested art form.

And then you get music as therapy.

People pay a lot of money to go talk to someone about their problems. They think that telling a stranger about their bad days and troubled thoughts will help them cope. Not me, throw some Rock and Roll on and I'm cured of all illnesses.

I have made a funny observation over the years. I'm sure you've noticed but I'd doubt your thoughts on it are the same as mine. You know, how people think soft, relaxing music will help them calm down if they're in a bad mood. Some people get a little worked up, have a shout and then think they have to spend the next 2 hours listening to James Blunt, or Celine Dion. Some soft, soppy shit that they think will get them in a good mood again.

James Blunt or Celine Dion would get me in a *bad* mood. Make me want to kill someone—preferably James Blunt or Celine Dion.

I couldn't be more different.

If I find myself feeling a little low, down in the dumps, I'll whack on the most rockingly-loud, hard-arse metal you can imagine. I'll head bang hard and before I know it I'm smiling bright.

Rock and Roll is my medicine.

'Sex, Drugs and Rock n' roll'. I lived by those rules far too many times in my life.

The only clichéd thing I find in Rock and Roll is the whole 'death of a band member' speech.

Why is it that every time a member of a band, any band, dies, the band come out with the following speech—'We're going to continue on. It's what such and such would've wanted'. Just once I wish they'd say 'You know, such and such would've wanted us to stop but, fuck it, we're still alive so we're going to keep going'.

I'm sure there's a band out there somewhere that has a member that's said 'You know, If I die, you better not keep going because without all of us, this isn't a band'.

These are just my thoughts. My opinions. It definitely doesn't mean they're right. Stop me anytime you want. Okay, you win. Next topic. Oh, does it have to be this one?

CHAPTER 13
. . . .

Strike 1

So, as I said before I got carried away with Rock and Roll. I was 18 years old. Had no job and hanging around Scotty.

Behind Scotty's place there lived a couple and their two kids. The guy drove a tow truck and the mother . . . well, I don't know, she did something. They had a boy and a girl. Two working parents and a child of each sex—the perfect family. It seemed that everyone around me had the perfect family. My house was the exception on the block.

Scott hated them for that exact reason, which I never got because Scotty had the perfect family, minus a sister. Go figure.

From the outside looking in they didn't come across as rich (I later found out that they were anything but). So I don't know how Scotty got it in his head that they were loaded. But that's how it started.

Now as I've already told you, Scotty had a knack for coming up with risky, daring . . . let's be honest—stupid ideas. We've had the one where he had me stuff lollies into my pockets at the local store. One I didn't tell you about that ended with a cracked windscreen and me having to endure another lesson. And of course, the only one I'm thankful for, snatching a purse from a little, old lady.

Well this one topped them all. As we were getting older it was probably inevitable (Websters Dictionary page 256) that the ideas would get more outrages. More dangerous. More stupid!

The first line spelt trouble. 'Man, I've got a great idea. If you're game?'

Scotty and I were sitting on his back steps, overlooking the Cook's place. He was all excited as he spoke.

'What?' I knew it wouldn't be good. Scotty's ideas never were.

He looked out over the back yard, straight into the Cook's house. I followed his gaze.

'I bet you those guys have a shit load of good stuff in their house'.

I didn't get it. Like I said before, they looked anything but rich.

'Who, the Cooks?'

Scotty gave me a look that said "I don't care what they're name is". His response almost said exactly that.

'You know them? Love thy fucking neighbour!'

'Sure I know them. My Mum talks to them.

'Of course she does. So tell me this; has she been inside the house?'

'Plenty of times'.

Scotty's enthusiasm lifted by a thousand.

'And what did she say? Was there a lot of expensive shit?'

What? Did he expect my Mum to scope out all the houses she went in? I could imagine it now. Mum would walk into the house of a new friend and open the conversation with; 'So, what are the more expensive stuff you have? You know, for if I decide to steal anything. I want to go straight to the good stuff'.

'She didn't say anything'.

'We should break into their place. You know that they go somewhere every second Saturday night. Right? So . . . the place will be deserted. This Saturday!'

I looked at Scotty with a blank expression. 'You want me to break into their house?'

'I want *us* to break into the place. We'll do it together'.

Sure because we're a happy couple that does everything together. What the Fuck did he want me to say?

'You and me?'

'Yep'.

'Break into the Cook's house?'

'Yep'.

'Why?'

'Why the fuck do you think—to steal some shit! Get some money so we can go hit the town. Why do I got to spell everything you for you?'

"Because you're a moron and I don't know why I ever started, and continued to hang around you", was what I wanted to say. The words came out different though.

'No, you don't. I was just checking'.

'Right, so you're in?'

This was the part where an Angel would perch on your left shoulder and a Devil would take residence on you right and duke it out between them. The angel would tell you all the reasons why you shouldn't do the stupid thing that you were about to do. And the Devil would come along and tell you why the Angel was such a Pussy and that you should definitely do that stupid thing you were thinking about. I always thought of it like you see in the cartoons. The Angel would show up, all dressed in white—Good Guy—and tell you that it was wrong to do it. You'll only get hurt and hurt those around you. You should turn around and leave. Then the Devil would come, pull out a cartoon-sized bazooka and blow the angels head clean off.

And as was becoming more and more the norm, the Devil won.

'Sure'.

Scotty hugged me. He hugged me because I was willing to break into a house with him. Dickhead! The way some people get their kicks huh?

Who was I to talk?!

'Fuck yeah man! Let's do this!'

I faked a smile and went along with his enthusiasm.

Truth is I was actually starting to like doing this bad, stupid stuff. I got a kick out of it.

We sat there for another hour planning the big heist. Scotty's Mum came to the back steps a few times to ask what we were doing. We told her that we were just chatting. She jokingly commented on the second visit 'I hope you're not planning to get into any trouble?' We laughed and waved her away. If only she knew.

That was Wednesday afternoon.

By Saturday evening the plan was still the same. Scotty ran over the plan a million times since Wednesday. We knew it by heart. Ever little detail. It wasn't the hardest plan to remember. We would wait until the family left, jump the fence, wedge a window open, climb in, grab the shit and get out. Easy.

I met Scotty in my back yard as soon as we saw the Cook's car leave. He was decked out in the clichéd Break and Enter costume: Black shoes, black pants, black shirt, black jacket and balaclava as he ran over to where I stood beside the laundry (Back in those days the laundry was outside the house, generally at the bottom wf the back stairs).

My B&E costume was the same as my sitting-on-the-couch-doing-Fuck-all clothes—Cargo shorts (Army camouflage), Black Band Shirt and Black Chuck Taylors. I didn't have a balaclava. Amateur.

We stood in the dark for less than a minute before Scotty broke the silence. 'Let's go then'.

And just like that my criminal life begun.

We slithered over the fence between my place and the Cooks. Scotty made me go first as he pulled the balaclava over his head.

'Where's your mask?'

'I don't have one', I replied as i turned to see Scotty jump the fence.

'Every criminal needs a balaclava'.

It hadn't occurred to me yet that we were criminals. Maybe after that night but not before.

'I'll look into it'.

We rounded the house until we found a window that was slightly open. Scotty picked up a stick from the yard and stuck the sharp end between the window and its frame. The stick broke and went falling to the ground.

I laughed as he had to step back to avoid being hit.

'Very fuckin' funny!' he snarled through gritted teeth as he picked up another branch and tried again. This time the window opened enough so that we could get our hands in.

Scotty pulled the window all the way open then turned to me. I was standing behind him with hands in my pockets, scratching my nether regions. I had no idea what was expected of me. This was my first B&E. I'm sure it was Scotty's too. At least I guessed it was. He did seem to know what he was doing though as if it was instinct.

My accomplice gripped the window ledge and looked over his shoulder toward me. 'Give me a boost'.

I walked over, crouched beside him low enough so that he could stand on my now entwined hands dangling in front of me. With one boost he was through the window and into the dark room.

I gripped the window ledge and tried to lift myself up. It didn't work. Whilst still dangling from the ledge I tried to grip my feet on the plaster wall to get some traction. That didn't work either. The wall was so slippery that I may as well have been trying to grip an ice wall in thongs. I was running on the spot on a vertical wall.

Where the hell was Scotty?! Why isn't he lifting me up?

Then my question was answered.

Scotty's head poked out through the curtain. 'What are you doing? Why didn't you go around to the back door?'

I forgot that part of the plan.

I let go of the ledge and dropped to the ground in a heap.

Scott chuckled as he pulled his head back in. 'Go to the back door. I'll let you in.'

Right.

Back door.

Got it.

When I got to the back door it was wide open. I walked in. I was in the Cook's kitchen. It looked like any other kitchen—Stove, Oven, Sink, Fridge, Freezer, Table and Cupboards. I don't know where Scotty got the impression that this family was loaded.

Scotty was standing at the fridge when I walked in. His body was silhouetted by the light from the fridge. Interesting place to start.

'What are you doing?'

'Seeing what alcohol the old man's got'. He moved away from the fridge with a beer in each hand. 'And look at that. Cold beer'.

Slamming the fridge closed, Scotty threw a beer at me. It hit me and smashed on the floor. Glass scattered all over the floor.

'What the fuck are you doing?!'

'I didn't know you were going to throw a bottle at me. I wasn't expecting it'.

Scotty sat his beer on the kitchen table and started down the hallway. 'Let's see what they've got'.

I looked all around me. I was surrounded by broken beer bottle. 'Are we just going to leave this here?'

'It's not my house. I'm not cleaning it up'. With that he went into a room, out of sight.

I started to make my way toward the hallway. Broken bottle crunched under my feet with each step. The noise was amplified by the silence.

I finally made it past the glass carpet and hurried my steps down the hallway.

And that's when the front door swung open.

'Hang on. I just need to change my bra'. Mrs Cook burst through the door with her blouse half open.

I was down the hall and out the back door before she was half way through the lounge room.

Scotty must've still been in the room when I heard the scream. Mrs Cook had walked straight into her bedroom. The room Scotty was in rummaging through drawers.

I don't know what scared her more—the stranger in her bedroom or the fact that she was wearing nothing but a skirt and high heels when she ran into him. I think the former. But only just.

As I ran through the backyard towards the fence I saw Mr. Cook dart from his car, straight up the front porch and into the house.

More screaming.

I jumped the fence and laid flat on my stomach amongst the high grass in my backyard. I looked over towards the Cooks where lights were being switched on. My heart was beating at a rate beyond anything I'd ever experienced.

I must've been laying there for an hour when the Police car pulled into the driveway belonging to the Cooks.

The screaming had ceased after about five minutes. I could only imagine what the next 55 minutes were like.

Mrs. Cook brought the kids in from the car as Mr. Cook watched over Scotty.

Sitting at the kitchen table with his captor, Scotty didn't say a word as they waited for the Police. That time had arrived.

It was no more than ten minutes before the Police escorted Scotty out of the house and into the back of their patrol car. He had his hands tucked behind his back. They had hand-cuffed him.

The flashing lights on top of the Police car had attracted a crowd. The neighbours were out in their yards watching the show.

I looked over into Scotty's yard as the Police car pulled out of the Cook's driveway. His Mum was leaning against the fence talking to my Mum. I could hear their conversation.

'I wonder what happened?' Scotty's Mum was whispering as the flashing lights faded into the distance.

'I don't know', was all my Mum could offer in response.

'I hope their all safe'.

'I'm sure they are', my Mum started 'there was no ambulance'.

'That's true'.

The Cooks were standing on their front porch. They had noticed that many of the neighbours were standing in their yards watching what was going on. They walked inside their house, closed the door and turned off the front porch light.

I waited until my Mum had gone back into the house to make my move. I stood up, brushed the dirt and grass from my shirt, ran around to the front door and walked in as casually as I could.

My Mum was watching TV by this time.

Suzie was asleep on the couch.

'Where have you been?'

"I—I was—I've been-'

'Is Scott with you?'

Ah-Umm-He's-'

'You're alone?'

'Yeah I'm alone. I don't know where he is tonight'.

'Ok. Well do you know what happened next door?'

'No. Where?'

'Over at the Cooks. There was a Police car there. We saw them take someone out to the car in cuffs'.

I went through the lounge room, down the hallway and into my room. 'I don't know'.

After a hot shower I went straight to bed.

The next morning I was awoken by a stern knocking on my door. I didn't answer at first, thinking it was my Mum but when the knocking persisted I shouted out 'What?'

My door opened and I saw my Mum standing there. I took me a moment to notice the two blue-uniformed people standing behind her.

My head slumped. I kicked the sheets off, swung my legs over the side of the bed and stood up. I could tell by the look my Mum was giving me that she now knew why the Cops were over at the Cooks last night.

And how did the Police know? Scotty told them.

I was ratted out by Scotty.

Apparently he didn't want to take the rap on his own. He told the Police that it was all my idea and that I forced him to do it with me.

Can you believe that?!

The Police took me away.

Mum was crying. Suzie was crying because Mum was.

They did me a favour by not putting my hands in cuffs. So they say.

I was down at the Police Station for the entire day. Answering the same questions a thousand times.

'Whose idea was it?'

'How did you get inside?'

'Had you been in there before?'

'What is your home life like?'

'What did you take from the house?'

Those same questions over and over again. They didn't even word them differently to try and catch me out. It was the same 5 questions asked exactly the same way, word for word, time upon time upon time.

I answered them all truthfully.

The outcome—I got 300 hours community service and a fine for $650.

Scotty got the same.

Mum was disappointed in me, as you'd expect. When I got home from the Police Station she was feeding Suzie at the kitchen table. I sat down at my place where Mum had my meal waiting and started to eat.

Suzie got off her seat, ran around my side and jumped on my lap.

Mum told her to get back on her seat. 'Back to your seat Suzie dear'.

I hugged Suzie, patted her bum and told her to go finish her dinner. I didn't make eye contact with Mum the whole time.

Eventually she spoke to me. 'So, what happened?'

I told her everything, from when we planned the B&E right up until I left the Police Station.

'So where are you going to do the Community service?'

I hadn't thought of that. Where would I do it? Where would you want to spend 300 hours working and not get paid a cent?

'I don't know. I'll find somewhere.'

And I did.

I would do my Community service at the Church that Grace went to.

The last thing I thought I'd find there was God.

And I was right. I didn't.

I found something better.

. . . And worse.

INTERMISSION
. . . .

When I decided to try and write my story I started with a list of topics I wanted to discuss. These topics ranged from everything between 'School days' and 'Girls' to 'Death' and 'Redemption'. Some of these we have already covered, the others you will read about further on (That's if you decide to keep reading).

These topics became the subjects of what would essentially be the Chapters of my life.

The reason I bring this up is because we are now half way through the Topics that I want to talk about. Or near enough.

You've made it half way. Congratulations.

I know it's probably hard to listen to someone you don't know blabber on about his life page after page. I just hope that you read it, learn from my mistakes and take in enough information to prevent you, or anyone you know, doing the same.

But we know each other a little but by now, right?

So let's do a recap. As they say.

I'm 18 years old. I left School the day I turned 16 and have done nothing since. I have no job and have never even looked for one. (Fuck, I'm turning into that guy I use to call "Dad").

I have a loving Mother that I try my hardest to be good for. I don't always succeed but I do try.

And I have a beautiful little sister—Susie. She's 4 now and means the world to me. I'd do anything for her. All she has to do is ask.

I had a poor upbringing. Through no fault of my Mother. We just didn't have much. It was that simple. It was nothing unusual back then. Still isn't. Poverty's all around. Most people are just too ashamed and try to hide it. It always shows its ugly self in the end but.

I lost two great friends, one of them the best I ever had, the day after my 18th birthday. I started using that as an excuse for doing wrong, bad shit.

I went from an innocent, quite, shy 9 year old boy to a mouthy, arrogant, loser 18 year old man. And I didn't even notice. Naive. (That word).

My story isn't anything grand or spectacular.

And I'm sure you'd agree.

I certainly don't think it's worth telling any more than *your* story. What I've done, and been through may be common occurrences. I'm sure a lot of it has happened to hundreds, thousands, no, millions of people.

For me, the difference is the whole good guy/bad guy scenario. Every story has a good guy and a bad guy, right? You can always tell them apart. Know which is which. And that's got a lot to do with their costume.

Look at Ninja movies. The good guys are always in white, while the bad guys are in black. Easy to tell apart. Black and white.

Superhero movies are similar. The good guy always has some fancy costume with bright colours, flaring capes that have a big letter on them and trendy masks. And what does the bad guy generally have—a black suit. Sometimes he may carry a cane. But he never limps.

My life has never been so black and white. I tend to play the good guy as well as the bad guy. At different times I will be one or the other. Sometimes I may even be both all rolled into one. And that was the main problem: I didn't always know which one I was being. Or trying to be.

I can tell you though, as is the standard Rock and Roll costume that I tend to stick to, I am almost always in black.

Another thing and it may be the main thing that splits the good guys from the bad—Consequences. Or more specifically, realising that there is such a thing. A good guy is exactly that because he, or she, knows that for everything you do there are consequences. If you do something wrong you will be punished. A bad guy, or girl—person, doesn't think about the consequences. They act on impulse and don't think about the effects. All they care about is doing wrong and reaping the benefits—if any.

So are you up to speed? Did the recap help?

Now, I still saw the other guys from the gang occasionally but not as much as I should've. And I was still spending too much time with Scotty.

But let's pick up where the last topic dropped off. Just for the sake of flow.

Listen to me, moving on as if you have already decided that you will keep reading. Am I that naive?

Chapter 14

Religion

I need to remind you about the advice my Mum gave me in regards to Politics: Don't argue about something that you know absolutely nothing about. You'll never win.

Well that could definitely be applied to me and Religion.

I knew nothing about it.

I mean I knew the basics—God created the world. Jesus came along. Jesus was God's son. Jesus died because everyone in the world was, and always will be, bad. God sent Jesus back to prove some point. No one got it.

And now people worship Jesus because of this.

Now, I've already told you that I don't believe in God. I don't believe in Fate, or Destiny or any of that garbage.

And I've also mentioned that I'm a believer of the Big Bang Theory. I think the world, the Universe and everything we see was created by one singular event in time where something happened that caused a cataclysmic catastrophe. And out of that event . . . stuff was made.

Simple as that. Why complicate things by making up false idols?

I mean, which theory is easier to believe: One guy is to blame for creating every single thing that we see, or, an event occurs—a freakish occurrence that created life, and over time that life evolved into what we are today?

Pretty obvious to me who's lying.

Anyway . . .

This part of my story isn't about Religion as such as it's about what I found when I was in the house of God and for the 18 months that I pretended to believe in it.

I showed up for my first day of Community Service just in time for the Sunday morning mass. If it wasn't bad enough that I had to do the Community Service, I had to show up for the first day on a Sunday morning. Talk about paying your debt to society.

Grace had organised a meeting for me with the Pastor of the Church. In fact, Grace had organised everything. She convinced the Pastor to let me do my service at their church.

I owe Grace for so much in my life.

Standing outside the Church I could hear the singing. Even from the street you could tell that the people in the Church were passionate. Their singing drowned out the traffic passing by.

I took this opportunity to slip into the back row of the Church un-noticed.

The sight that met me was an eye-opener. People singing aloud, arms raised up in the air as if they were expecting to have to hold up the falling ceiling, and they all had their eyes closed.

I noticed Grace straight away. I could see the back of her. You can't miss that purple hair. She was sitting up in the first row with arms raised. Those little legs couldn't stand for too long.

The pastor was directly in front of her up on his little stage, shielded by a big, wooden podium in the shape of a cross. He was dressed all in white with a purple scarf draped around his neck.

To the left of the Pastor, on the little stage, a band was set up. There was a guy at the back sitting at a set of drums. You could barely hear the drums he was tapping them that soft. To his right there was another guy playing an acoustic guitar. That I could hear. To the left of the drummer there was a third guy playing a bass guitar. He was dressed like a Rasta man—totally out of place. At the front of the stage there were two microphones set up. The microphone on the left was being used by a plump lady who was putting all her might, and spit, into it. There was a microphone on the right at the front of the stage and standing behind that was a girl tapping a tambourine against her slim, smooth thigh.

She was tall and thin with long, straight black hair that shone brighter than a lighthouse beacon. On this particular day, the first time I laid eyes on the dark-haired Goddess, she was wearing one of those thin summer dresses that swirled around in even the slightest breeze. It was a creamy colour with little floral patterns splattered all over and had small straps that went over her shoulders. The top was sleeveless and hugged her petite upper body like a singlet.

I was instantly smitten. Full of Lust.

I just wanted to get my hands on her.

And to my delight, Grace knew her.

When the singing stopped and the mass was over, the stunning Vixen walked off the stage and straight over to where Grace was still sitting. She leaned down and hugged Grace. When she pulled away Grace stood up and made a conscience move to scan the room. At this point she turned and saw me and made a waving sign to call me over. I had stood up to stretch.

I waved back in recognition and made my way down the centre aisle of the Church. (I got to walk down the aisle. Hilarious).

Grace hugged me when I got to her, as she always did. The tall angel stood to the side smiling.

When Grace let go she grabbed my arm and faced me towards the sweet smelling female to my left.

After our introductions Grace led me out to the back of the Church to meet the Pastor.

Her name was Beth. The first thing I noticed when I was standing there being introduced to her was her figure. Talk about stopping traffic, she could've grounded all planes. The material of her dress was so thin that you could virtually see the curves and bumps of her obviously stunning body.

The one thing I didn't notice was the wedding ring on her long, perfectly shaped finger.

Why would it surprise me that a girl as gorgeous as Beth, who was a part of a church community would be married?

As I stood there talking to the Pastor, listening as he told me what I would be doing, all I could think about was Beth.

She was . . . my thoughts.

I caught enough of what the Pastor said to know that my first job was to mow the grounds of the church.

Grace said goodbye to me when Beth came out to retrieve her. Apparently Beth was Grace's lift to and from church.

Why hadn't I ever seen her at Grace's?

I spent the rest of that afternoon cutting grass and picking up branches.

All of a sudden I was looking forward to church. I had to go there every Sunday morning and Wednesday afternoon. And I can tell you that I was there 20 minutes early on the following Wednesday.

And would you believe it . . . she wasn't there.

Apparently she went on Sunday mornings and evenings. Never on a Wednesday.

So I slaved through the Wednesday, replacing old flowers in the church.

I went to visit Grace every day from Thursday to Saturday. I had one purpose for being there: find out all I can about Beth.

Grace knew a fair bit. Beth played in the church band at each service Sunday morning and afternoon and she was also an active member of the church committee. She lived a few suburbs away and worked as a Secretary for some big Law firm in the city. She was two years older than me and had been married for three years. Her Husband's name was Karl and he went to the Sunday afternoon service. I guess I'll meet him this Sunday cause I planned on going to both services.

But then something unexpected happened.

Really unexpected!

I was over visiting Grace Friday night and Beth showed up. She was alone and on her way home from work. Her and I got to talking and kept at it even after Grace went to bed.

Grace sensed something was up. I could tell. She hugged Beth goodnight then came over to me. As she hugged me she said one simple word, a word I was having more and more trouble with—'behave'.

I smiled at her and bid her goodnight.

Beth and I were alone.

What was going on? I had no idea.

Why is this beautiful, church-going, *married* girl sitting with me alone, in a dark kitchen at 10pm on a Friday night?

I decided to not over-analyse it and just went with the flow.

We talked about so many things that night. She touched on the topic of Jesus and whether I believed in him. I didn't know how to answer it. I made a decision there and then to say that I did believe in Jesus. I mean, you have a beautiful creature smiling at you with come-hither eyes and asks you a simple question that was way too easy to lie about. What're you going to do?

By the end of the night I had invited her to a day out. The following day, I suggested. Just her and I. She said yes with no hesitation. I even offered her to bring her Husband. She said no, he wouldn't want to come along.

I didn't know what to do when she was leaving. Do you kiss a married girl goodnight? A married, god-loving girl no less.

I hugged her and followed her apple-shaped bum as it got in the car. That arse, I still picture it now. Perfect. *The most perfect rear end you would ever see.* She drove away waving and I returned the gesture.

I couldn't sleep that night. All I could think about was that I was going to spend the next day with God's most beautiful creation.

Can you tell that I was smitten?

I was also confused. I mean, I was far from a good guy, but wanting a married woman, that was a new emotion even for me.

How would I handle it? The same way any red-blooded bloke would—we had an 18 month affair.

How did it start? Our day in the park.

Beth met me at Grace's place the following morning. I was awake, showered, dressed and at our meeting spot before the roosters sung.

Grace was waiting for me at the kitchen table. At least it looked that way, but she was always having her first cup of tea at this time of the morning.

I was three hours early to meet Beth mind you.

I walked in through the back door, poured myself a cup and sat at the kitchen table.

'You make sure to be careful, dear'. It didn't take Grace long to get to her point.

I sipped my tea and looked up at her, pulling the cup away with a slurp. 'Sorry?'

'Beth. Be careful with her'.

I didn't know what she was getting at.

'What do you mean?'

'She has a way'.

'With God, yeah I know'.

Grace looked at me with poppy-dog eyes as if to say "Oh dear, surely you're not that naive?"

There's that word again. I should get it tattooed onto my forehead.

'No love. She has a way with Men. Men other than her husband. Don't get me wrong, she's a wonderful girl with a heart of gold, but in the church you hear things. Now they may not be true but you do see how people interact with the opposite sex. Beth is certainly drawn more to the men in the crowd then the ladies'.

This was exactly what I wanted to hear. My job was going to be half done before I even clocked in.

'Grace, I'm sure that's not true. She goes to church, is married and worships God like, like . . . well, like he's a God'.

In the back of my mind I was thinking "I wonder where the first place we'll have sex will be? The park maybe".

'Ok dear. Just be careful. That's all I'm saying. You don't want to get yourself in trouble in God's eyes, especially if it's with a married woman'.

'I promise I'll behave'.

Grace grinned at me and sipped her tea.

I finished my cup, rinsed it out and went out to sit on the front steps to wait for my visitor. I sat there for almost two hours waiting. Finally, her car pulled up.

Beth parked in the driveway and waved for me to get in the car.

I ran down the steps and hopped in the passenger seat. The smell of perfume rushed into my nostrils and tingled my senses immediately.

The day started with a lie. 'I hope you weren't waiting long?'

'Oh no. I just got there'.

I buckled my seatbelt and we drove off. From the moment the accelerator went down we got to chatting. There were no uncomfortable pauses, no stuttering, no struggles to make up conversation. We genuinely talked the whole way to the park. And it was all interesting—to me at least. Beth seemed to be enjoying it just as much.

Before I knew it we were at the Park and the car was unpacked.

I'm not going to go into every detail about the day. We chatted. We flirted. She touched my arm so many times I lost count. At one point she actually hugged me. I don't remember why. Does it matter?

We sat in the park for a few hours until Beth made an offer I couldn't refuse. 'Hey, let's go to my place'.

'Isn't your Husband home?' This was the first time he had been acknowledged. She seemed a bit put off by the question but quickly recovered.

'He's at work'.

And on that note we were in the car and on our way back to Beth's house. She made me drive, which I'd only dabbled in a few times. At the time, Mum was letting me drive her car on the occasion. I had only had my licence for about half a year but I was a good driver. I was sensible, which you probably find hard to believe but it's true.

The whole way back Beth rested a hand on my left leg. It never moved. If it were a hot iron I would've had a hole in my pants.

We got to her house, didn't bother to empty the picnic stuff from the car and went straight inside.

First point of stop was the bedroom.

I had many thoughts running through my head at the time: Why was she bringing me here? And to the bedroom straight away? Who was this chick? What is she doing? I wonder what colour her nipples were? And were they perky?

As she led me through to her bedroom Beth signalled for me to sit on the bed.

'I'm just going to take a shower', Beth commented as she walked into the suite.

'Sure'.

'Take your shoes off, lay down. It's ok. He won't be home for a while'.

"He??"

She didn't even use his name.

As the door to the bathroom closed I kicked off my shoes and lay back on the bed. It was soft and had about a thousand pillows on it. I nearly drowned when I leaned into them.

What was going on? Was I about to screw this chick? This good Christian girl? A married woman!

God I hoped so.

Beth walked out of the bathroom in an open robe—a tiny, red silk robe that barely covered her shoulders let alone anything else. Under the robe she was wearing lime green coloured lingerie. Her body looked amazing. Defined stomach. Perfect-sized, perky-looking breasts.

I hadn't died and gone to heaven, one of heaven's creatures had come to be.

She didn't muck around. This girl knew what she was doing. I was certain she had done this before. And not with her Husband, I mean.

She didn't hop on the bed, she hopped on me. Straddled me. One leg on each side of my body. Her robe flapped open revealing her beautiful hips.

We chatted, never mentioning what was going on. It's like she was diverting our attention from the reality of what we were doing.

I could tell she was struggling with something but.

'We don't have to do this'. I offered.

'No it's not that', she started 'I just know that if I kiss you once I'll want it more'.

I didn't see the problem there.

'So don't kiss me'.

'I want to'.

'So kiss me then'.

'I want to'.

'So what—'

I didn't finish that line. She was kissing me. Beth, this gorgeous, *drop-dead* gorgeous girl was kissing me. I didn't waste any time. I rubbed my hands over her shoulders, pulling down the robe in the process. It was flung off to the side with sheer urgency. I had my hands around those hips and was holding on for dear life.

An hour later we were lying side by side amongst the crumpled sheets not talking about what had just happened.

That's when it occurred to me "I hadn't found out the answer to my earlier question about her nipples. She kept her bra on the whole time. I got to explore every other inch of her body though.

Next thing I knew I was having to leave in case her Husband came home.

Get them in and out before the man shows up. She'd done this before. Surely.

I left and got a sensual kiss on my exit. We said our goodbyes.

'I guess I'll see you at Church Sunday'.

'I guess you will', she replied.

And with that I started the long walk to the nearest train station.

I later learnt that there was a term that summed up what happened. Beth penned it. She said that there was no way we weren't going to have sex. As soon as I agreed to go to her place it was inevitable that we'd hit it. And why do you think that is? Because when I agreed to the Invitation, it gave "Implied Consent" for her to throw herself at me.

Funny hey?!

The things people will come up with to justify what they do.

Church Sunday went by without any fanfare. Beth acted like the perfect Church-going, God-loving person that everyone thought her to be.

Everyone except me.

This girl was living two *extremely different*, separate lives and I was the only one who knew it.

I'm sure Grace was well aware, though she never said anything to anyone. Bless her.

And she kept her opinion to herself for the next 6 months while I worked off my Community Service.

I had totally forgot that I was there as punishment. If this was punishment, bring it on.

By the time my community service had been paid in full, I was going to Church with Beth, and her Husband on a regular basis.

That's right. We were having an affair right under the nose of the Church, all her friends, God, and her Husband. No one suspected a thing.

Beth and I would get together any chance we had to indulge in the physical side of our affair. We had a regular spot up at a local look-out where we would meet up. I was using Mums car more and more and, in turn, was getting better at driving.

We would meet at the look-out and I'd get into her car. She'd be sitting there waiting for me. We'd always chat for a little while before she'd hike her skirt up and unzip my fly. On these meets she never wore underwear. What a turn on that was. She crawled over to where I sat and spread her legs over my groin.

We'd go at it like animals for a long time, give her a chance to wind down after we were done then we'd go our separate ways.

It always amused me to think that every time her Husband sat in the passenger seat he may have been sitting on the remains of one of our encounters.

Kind of disgusting to mention that, wasn't it? Sorry. It'll be omitted before anyone else sees it. I'll leave it there for now just for my amusement.

Do you know the worst thing but? I actually felt like I had to start saying I believed in God. Maybe that was her plan. Sex, an affair, was her way of converting people over to God. Tell you what, if word got round about that, she'd have her Church bulging at the seams.

I was lying about believing in God and Jesus and all that shit just so I could continue this affair with Beth.

She started taking me to her Church groups. I don't know what you'd call them. It'd be where a group of young adults got together and shared in the love of God. They'd put on dinners. Play Religious games. Sit around praying and asking for forgiveness.

I became friends with all of these people and none of them knew my real intentions for being there.

They were fucking oblivious!

As this was going on I didn't notice that Mum had a new man visiting her.

His name was Nathan and I've gotta tell you, straight off the bat, he was a nice bloke.

The day I met him, Nathan pulled into the driveway with music coming out of the car. It was John Lennon.

Before Mum could even introduce us I was asking him 'Was that Cold Turkey?'

'Sure was', he replied.

Mum smiled as she walked down the path to greet him.

'Darling, this is Nathan. Nathan, this is my son I told you about'.

Nathan held out his hand and I shook it. Firm grip.

'You know your Lennon'.

'I know music', I confidently replied.

"Good guy" was my first thought. Nathan had that feel about him. I knew he meant well. I was satisfied that Mum was in good hands. If that was what was happening?

I turned my attention to Mum 'I need to talk to you'.

She looked at me whilst welcoming Nathan 'What is it?'

I looked at Nathan, then back to Mum 'In private?'

Mum looked to Nathan us if asking what to do next. Nathan took it upon himself to respond.

'Hey, why don't I head home? I've got things to do.'

'Are you sure? But you just got here.'

I felt guilty 'I didn't mean for you to leave.'

'That's all right. I've got things to do.'

Nathan leant in and kissed Mum on the cheek.

'Come back for dinner.'

I agreed that he should.

'Okay' Nathan replied.

As Nathan walked to his car, I followed Mum inside.

'He seems nice.'

'He is dear.'

'Is it serious?'

'It's getting that way'.

We walked inside the house and sat on the couch.

'Now, what is it dear?'

CHAPTER 15

Untitled

I told Mum the whole story about me and Beth. She was shocked but not that surprised. She didn't really have that much to say about it. That's the good thing about my Mum—She didn't judge.

I told her about how we met. Where we met. What we'd done. Everything we'd done. I mean *everything*.

She had one piece of advice to give me—"Be careful". That was it.

I thought I was being more then careful. None of her friends knew. Her Husband didn't know. I'd even been introduced to her Parents and they were as clueless as the rest.

The affair had been going for over a year now and it wasn't looking like slowing up any time soon. I was a part of her life. We were in love. We had actually admitted our love for each other.

This put me in a jam. I loved a girl that I couldn't have in the way I wanted. I'd come to the conclusion that I had found the girl of my dreams. I had tracked down the person I was meant to spend the rest of my life with.

The only problem was that some other guy had found her first. I was beaten to the punch.

And she was a devout Christian. What're you going to do? Those Christian folk. When they mate, they mate for life.

Strangely enough though, I never tried to make her leave her Husband. Maybe, deep down, I knew it was only a fling. On the surface I thought it was love and all that jazz but I knew, again, deep down, that eventually the bubble would burst.

We were heading into our 18th month of the affair and Beth's conscience finally kicked in.

Damn it!!!

During the relationship Beth tried a few times to lay the guilt trip out. The guilt was never meant to come from me. And trust me, it didn't.

One time we were in a park, there was a big pond in the middle and we were sitting on a bridge that went across it.

Beth was arguing that "what we are doing is wrong and people would get hurt". I don't know why it took her over a year to figure this out. I knew before we'd even kissed.

Bit slow on the uptake.

I laid on any charm that I might have had. Convincing her to continue following her lust, before I knew it we were in the front seat of her car making love.

That's another thing. We'd stopped calling sex "sex". We'd upgraded to "Making Love".

So we got through that scare and continued on in our ways for a further 6 months.

And then she hit me with the bombshell.

Beth confessed that I wasn't her first affair. She told me a story about how she used to live next to a guy that had a thing for her. I don't remember his name. We'll call him . . . Mr. A.

Well, Mr. A was some other nationality that I also don't remember. Not that that matters but I thought I'd throw it in.

Beth told me about their affair. She claimed that ours was different. She didn't have feelings for him like she did for me. She didn't "love" him.

I asked her why it happened and she said, wait for it, "Because he was there".

How do you like that?!

This Christian girl, little-miss-perfect, had cheated on her husband with the guy next door out of convenience.

It didn't bother me though. After all, I was the one screwing her at the moment. Well, me and her Husband.

Maybe it did bother me but because that was about the time we started pulling apart.

I started noticing things about Beth that weren't too attractive. Not physical things. Damn, there wasn't a single blemish on that body. Trust me, I checked.

The main problem I noticed—let's call it a trait of her character that I didn't much like—She was very manipulative (I won't tell you the page of the Dictionary that appears on. Look it up).

This girl could bat an eye lid and get anything she wanted.

Girls say they don't use their looks and bodies to get their own way. That's rubbish!

The end was in sight. I thought it best to be ready for the heartbreak.

It was strange—my relationship (???) was coming to an end, while Mum's was getting more and more serious.

Over the course of my affair with Beth, Mum and Nathan had gone from weekend get-together's to mid week sleepovers to full-time live in. Nathan had moved in with Mum, Suzie and I. Mum had never been happier.

Suzie too.

Because Nathan had come into Suzie's life at such a young age she clung onto him like glue. Not far from being called Dad, Nathan absolutely adored her. I couldn't blame her. I wish I had a male figure like him around when I was growing up. My life may have been so different. No use harping on that kind of thing.

I was finding it harder and harder to contact Beth. Whenever I called her she'd be out somewhere. She never said where or who with, just out. I knew it wouldn't be with her Husband as he'd be at work.

I automatically thought the worse.

That's the strangest part, I guess. Here was this girl that I was jealous of because she may be out with another guy, and she was married. She wasn't even mine to be jealous over.

Can you figure it out? No, seriously, can you because I can't?

Whenever she called me I still jumped at her beckon though. She would twist the situation until I felt guilty about something. I don't know what, but it was something.

And then one day she cut all ties.

We got together one day and went out to the local shops. We sat down to eat lunch and she spilled the beans.

'I can't do this anymore', she started 'this is not what God has in store for me'.

I knew she'd bring him into it.

'I have lost my way. I thought that I knew how to live my life but I'm wrong. God knows what I want and he knows what's good for me. I have to follow the path that he lays out for me. I need to give my life back to The Lord'.

I wasn't buying any of it. And do you want to know why? Because of what she said next.

'I have to accept that I am addicted to Sex. I don't know what it is. I just enjoy Dick (Her words). And I don't always mean that of my Husband'.

There it was. She was a sex-addict. I could've diagnosed her with that disease.

'I have to tell my Husband about us'.

This shocked me. I thought she'd take it to her grave.

It was my turn to respond. 'Are you going to tell him about Mr. A?'

Beth looked up from the table and stared blankly.

'No'.

Of course not!

'Why?'

'That was a long time ago, and it's different to what we did'.

'It's still cheating'.

This ended our last ever meal together.

Beth pushed her plate to the middle of the table, stood up and walked away, but not before turning to me.

'You know I love my Husband and I have problems that I have to deal with'.

And with that she was gone. I watched that fine arse sway for the last time.

Now do you want to know the funniest thing: I found out not long after that she had got together with another guy virtually straight after she left that lunch. She started seeing him whilst she and I were still she and I. I don't know his name. Who cares what it was.

I also heard that there was another guy, some friend she'd had since childhood that was madly in love with her. This guy made a move on her one night when they were at her house. The Husband was down stairs. She didn't kiss him back but at the same time, she didn't stop it. Apparently this guy had followed her when she moved interstate. He uplifted his life to stay near her. The Husband was oblivious to him too.

And she only told her Husband about me.

That's who I feel sorry for nowadays—The Husband.

Beth, I couldn't care less about you now.

She was a lying, manipulative bitch.

Fuck her! Fuck you!

The only time I think about her these days is when I need fuel to stoke the fire. On a lonely night when the dirty mags aren't doing the job I'll lie back and think about the dirty stuff her and I use to do and I'm done in two minutes.

She may have been a child of God but I can tell you this: Any time she was around me and was on her knees it certainly wasn't to prey. She had *me* calling his name, I can tell you that much too.

She most definitely was heaven sent.

That's if you believe in that place.

That's probably more of an accurate way to define my stand: It's not that I don't believe that there's a God it's just that I have no faith in the religion or the people that practice it.

Beth being a prime example.

I never got a "told you so" speech from Mum after it was all over.

Grace never led on if she ever knew about it. The whole time I thought we were hiding it from her well.

Turns out that old doesn't always mean blind.

But let's go back to the Husband. The poor bastard thinks he has the perfect, home-body, do-good, Christian wife. He thinks the sun shines out of her arse. Even after she told him about me, he didn't care. He forgave her and they are still together today.

It's what he doesn't know that makes me feel sorry for him. He has no idea that she was having an affair with their neighbour after being married for only two months. It doesn't occur to him that this childhood friend is following her from state-to-state because he's madly in love with his wife. And he definitely doesn't know that she had a brief affair with some other guy after her and I were over.

Oh well, all that is his problem now.

Good luck buddy.

I quickly found another mistress to help me forget about Beth.

A mysterious mistress known as . . .

CHAPTER 16

Dreaming (of Drugs)

I didn't discover Drugs until later in life. And I didn't exactly find them, more so someone introduced me to them. Which I guess is a more common way that people discover them.

I had lost touch with the guys I grew up with. After Craig's death we sort of went on to new things.

I had even neglected Scotty a bit while I was chasing Beth. We still saw each other but it was always brief. Let's just say that for those 18 months I was never around him long enough to get talked into doing anything stupid or illegal. I already had the stupid taken care of.

Scotty knew what I was doing with Beth. He urged me on most of the time. He used to joke that maybe he could have a turn after I was done. I think the joke would've been that she probably would've taken him up on it. I never told him that.

My whole life revolved around Beth for those 18 months. There was no time for the guys that I already hardly ever saw see, or Scotty. But since that phase of my life was over it was back to Scotty.

And then, one day I ran into David.

Scotty and I were walking out of a cinema at some shopping centre. I turned a corner and literally ran into him. My fists went up in defence straight away. When I pulled back to see my victim I noticed David standing there.

He looked different. There was something about him. His clothes were not that straight. A bit dirty. He kept biting his fingernails and darting his head from side to side in a paranoid-type manner. I don't think his shoes even matched.

Scotty nearly jumped on him in aide of me. I had to stop him.

'David, my man'.

He looked at me with glazed-red eyes.

'David, it's me man'.

David looked me up and down. He turned to the girl standing next to him. 'Get me a cheeseburger meal. A big one. And a Fillet burger. And a chocolate shake'.

The skinny thing by his side walked away without uttering a word.

'How have you been man?'

David looked over at Scotty then to me.

'All right.

'What're you up to? You remember Scotty right?'

'Sure', he said, nodding toward Scotty 'hey man'.

Scotty nodded back 'Fuck's it going?'

'All right'.

I remembered David being more talkative.

'Who's the chick?' I asked.

'Sally'.

'Nice'.

Nice? Scotty, what the hell? The chick was a skanky-looking, skeletal death-walker.

'We should do something man'. I was keen to catch up with one of the guys.

'Sure'.

'Where are you off to after this?'

Scotty had lost interest and was tapping his hands in a drum-like beat against the counter nearby.

'Sally and I are going home to smoke some shit'.

This got Scotty's attention. 'Smoke?'

'Yeah dude, smoke'.

'Smoke what. Cigarettes?'

I was close to 20 and still as naive as ever.

'Nah man, pot!'

My ears didn't register what they'd heard. I couldn't believe David would blurt that out in the middle of a packed food court.

I didn't believe David would say that period. He was never the type. None of the guys were. Sure we all did a few bad things in our youth: stole candy, drink alcohol, even sampled a cigarette or two, but none of us even dared try drugs.

Scotty was in. 'Really?!'

'Yeah. You want to come? You'll have to put in but'.

'Put in'. I didn't know the drug lingo.

'Yeah, pay for some. Put money in to buy a stick.

'Stick?'

'A stick of pot. It's the smallest amount you can buy. 25 bucks.'

He was more talkative now. We must have found a topic he was familiar with.

The problem was that it would be no time at all before I became familiar with it also.

Scotty and I followed David and his chemical praying mantis to some place where David went in and came back out five minutes later. He patted his groin and we kept walking.

'Got it.'

A few minutes later I was holding my first ever bong.

For anyone reading this that is a little lost at the moment, a "bong" is a device used to intake Marijuana. The two main types of bongs are what I will call 'The Poor-man's Bong' and 'The Posh Bong'.

The Poor-man's bong is usually made by using an empty, small orange juice or soft drink bottle as the chamber. Into that you would cut out a round hole in the side. Meanwhile you would go out to the front yard and cut off a small length of hose (anywhere between 5-10 centimetres is fine). Get a lighter and heat around the edges of the hole cut out previously. When the edges are hot take the piece of hose and jam it into the bottle. The edges of the hole should mould around the hose. What you're trying to do is get the hose into the bottle with the tip just above the bottom of the bottle, all the time keeping the bottle air-tight. Once you have the hose in—air-tight—you pierce a small hole into the bottle. Make the whole on the opposite side that the hose is sticking out of, close to the top of the bottle. Fill the bottom of the bottle with maybe about a centimetre of water. The hardest part is the cone. I have never made one in my life so I'll tell you to do what I always did—get someone else to make it. Once the cone is made you put it into the end of the hose that's sticking out of the bottle and there you have it—a fully-functional Brain masher. It should look like the diagram below.

THE POOR-MAN'S BONG

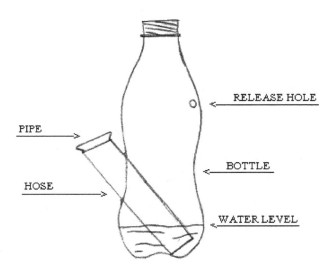

The Posh bong is similar except for the fact that you go to a store and buy it ready-made: Glass cylinder, metal pipe and proper stainless steel cone. If you want to see one of these just go to your closest Tobacco store. They'll have all kinds.

Regardless of your weapon of choice, the objective is the same—getting stoned.

The first bong I held was more like a homeless-man's bong. The water in it was dirty. Real dirty! It looked dirtier than the water from a mud bath. There were all kinds of stuff floating around in it: Hair, dirt, grass (of course), plastic. I think, if I remember correctly, there was even a fly basking in the filth.

It did the job but because after only one toke I was stoned out of my mind.

I coughed my lungs up after that first toke.

"Toke" is the term used to describe the act of inhaling the smoke. Like when you take a drag on a cigarette, instead, when you smoke a joint you don't take a drag you have a toke.

I am jumping ahead here.

Joint. A joint is the same as a cigarette. It looks similar in every way except that it has marijuana in it instead of tobacco.

So I put my mouth to the top of the bottle, lit the grass in the cone and watched the smoke swirl around in the bottle before it shot up the hose and down my throat.

The trick was not to swallow. You have to suck it in, let it linger for a few seconds then exhale. The more you smoke it, the longer you hold it in, the more stoned you get. That's the aim.

I held it in for a few seconds before the smoke came coughing out of me. My head instantly began to spin. I thought I was going to vomit. I dribbled a bit of spittle down my chin. I sucked too hard and some of the mud-bath water went in my mouth. It was the most disgusting taste I had ever experienced. To this day it hasn't been topped.

I fucken' loved it!

I was out of my head and in outer space off one toke of pot.

That's all it took. I was hooked.

Scotty too.

We left David's place later that day when his girlfriend started complaining that the drugs were going too quick. She didn't want to have to go to bed straight.

I thought that was a little desperate when I heard it. I later found out what she was referring to. Once you are hooked, addicted to marijuana, you can't get to sleep unless you are stoned senseless. And then you don't really fall asleep, you pass out. Or as the drug culture world call it—"Green Out".

And I was fast becoming part of that culture.

By this time in my life I had found a job. I was working for one of the leading Supermarkets in Australia. I won't say who to save their integrity.

If they have any to start with.

I worked Monday to Friday from 9 to 5.

I was the proper hard-working guy between these hours. It wasn't until knock-off time or the weekends that my darker side appeared.

It was more and more feeling like I was living two separate lives.

In one life I was a hard worker. I was a supportive son and big brother. I was a nice guy to Nathan.

The other life was at the far end of the spectrum though. I was a drug-taking, shop-lifting, no-caring loser.

As soon as 5 o'clock clicked over, so did my character.

I would go all day at work without even thinking about drugs. Not thinking about causing trouble. All I cared about was getting my work done and getting paid. But as soon as I clocked out that switch went off and my first thought was "Were can I get some pot?"

Most of my pay went on the debts I had built up during the week. Anything left over was used to buy more drugs. That's why I had to pay debts the next pay day. After my money had ran out the day after pay day, I had to get drugs on credit until my next pay. When you get drugs on credit they call it, in the drug culture world—Getting it on Tick. It was a savage loop.

This is what my life had come to—waking up, going to work, from work I'd go straight to a dealers house then I'd head home, get stoned, maybe have dinner, then pass out, only to wake up and do it all over again.

Every night for five years I went to bed stoned.

Most nights Scotty was right by my side egging me on and joining in. He wasn't working though so I was providing for two. Like a pregnant woman.

My life outside of work was being affected by my constant stoned-state.

I never spoke to Mum or Suzie. Nathan was always looking at me strangely. He knew what was going on.

I barely saw Grace anymore. Occasionally I would go visit her, help around the house to do things that she couldn't physically do. She would generally try to give me money for helping her, and as desperate as I was, I didn't, I *couldn't* take it.

I guess there was still some good left in me.

My room was my own little drug den.

My Wally Lewis poster had long ago been replaced by a Guns R Roses poster which in turn had been covered over with a poster showing all the different names for marijuana.

Pot. Green. Gunja. Skunk. Mary Jane. Spliff. Grass. Weed. Whacky Weed. Chronic.

It was my pride and joy.

Mum hated it.

I would take to locking myself in my room the second I got home and I wouldn't show my face until the next morning.

Scotty had started coming through the window. That way he could get stoned and not have to confront my family.

We would sit in my room with the incense candles burning away, listening to music.

Oh man, music took on a whole new meaning once I started listening to it while I was high. The Sgt. Peppers album was that much trippier. Jimi Hendrix was as savage as ever. Pink Floyd started making sense. It was awesome!

We would sit there and listen to tunes until I greened out and Scotty would exit through the window. Stage left.

It had become a ritual. We had no money, no girls but no cares. As long as we were high . . . that's all that mattered.

Drugs were my life.

I went from being on the other end of adultery to being a drug addict.

Bad to worse some may say. I didn't at the time.

Getting high was a good way to move on from Beth. And trust me, with the help of Mary Jane, she was forgotten about real quick. She was, after all, my new love. I had to have her.

But that changed one day.

I found myself starting to have to share my love between Drugs and another girl.

Her name was Vicki.

She was an addict too.

Only marijuana but.

To this day I have only ever been addicted to marijuana. I never graduated to anything heavier.

I did try speed a few times. I always drunk it but. I could never bring myself to sticking my arm with a needle. It never appealed to me. I hated the idea.

I would only use the acid when I was heading out to something where I knew being high would add to the event. Like a rock festival. I would drink down my capful of water laced with speed and be buzzing the whole time I was wandering around the festival listening to all the music that I grew up on and loved more than anything.

Besides my few dabbles into Speed it was all Marijuana for me.

Vicki was the same.

We ventured out to a few of those festivals together, both of us wasted off our mind and buzzing like bees with ADHD.

You didn't even need pot when you were buzzing on speed. It had no effect. It didn't stop us taking a few joints with us just in case. They always got put to use.

Back to Vicki.

One day Scotty and I went over to David's place to score. We knocked on the door and this short, blonde-haired girl answered. It wasn't David's girlfriend, I knew that right away.

Scotty and I shared a stare that we knew was our way of fighting for rights to this girl.

I kept staring at Scotty as this girl let us into the house. We said hi to David then sat down on the couch. There was a packed bong on the table so Scotty picked it up and smoked it. This hit a chord with the new girl. She went off in a tirade.

'What do you think you're doing? That was my cone'.

This startled Scotty. He looked at me and shook his head. This was his way of saying "She's all yours".

I think she was a bit forward for him.

Suited me fine.

Vicki was a little gem.

By the end of our visit I had convinced her to come over my house the next day and get high.

Little did I know that the lives of Vicki and I would become entwined from that day on.

CHAPTER 17

Girls—Part 2

Vicki was different from any girl I had ever met or been with. I could tell that straight away. For one I had a new drug companion.

Another thing . . . she got me. She really got me. I could be myself around her and that was fine. It was enough.

No manipulating. No lying. No faking. No pretending to be something we weren't.

I had found my soul mate.

Initially we bonded over drugs.

The first time Vicki came over to my place we didn't do much. We got high and listened to music.

Vicki loved Rock and Roll. And what guy doesn't like a girl that digs Rock n Roll? Tell me.

She knew all the words to every song on Appetite for Destruction. She even thought that the best song on the album was Nighttrain. My opinion also. We listened to Dr. Feelgood over and over. Kickstart my heart was the favourite there. She was just as much at home listening to Rubber Soul or Revolver.

Scotty started to get jealous because this time was generally reserved for him and me. I ignored him though because we'd still do our thing when Vicki wasn't around. I still went on late night strolls around the suburb with Scotty.

I just started making time to spend with Vicki. This girl had stolen my heart for no other reason except that we understood each other and got along. But that's what it's all about right?

I don't think I made a move until about the tenth time she came over.

Mum and Nathan were getting used to seeing her around.

Suzie was a little shy at first but she came out of her shell and Vicki would actually have them playing together.

That was another sign that she was perfect. She got along with my family almost as much as she did with me.

On the day's she wasn't over, Mum would question it. 'Where's Vicki today love?'

'She's got things to do.'

'Will she be here soon?'

Mum knew that if Vicki was coming over that meant another day without Scotty. She still didn't like the idea of me hanging out with him, especially after the Break and Enter escapade.

The night I finally made a move on Vicki was the most nerve-racking moment I had experienced at that point in my life.

It was one of the rare nights that both Scotty and Vicki were sitting with me in my room listening to the latest Metallica CD. We were stoned but not too stoned. I was buzzing, that's for sure. Scotty and I were sitting on the floor against my bed. Vicki was lying on the bed with her head and arm dangling over the side. Whilst Scotty was head banging to just about the greatest bridge in any Metallica song I had ever heard, I decided to make my move. I started playing with her hand. I was making light circle motions on her palm. She never looked at me but I could tell she was enjoying it. Her fingers stretched out so that I could stroke them. And I did. Scotty didn't even look our way. He was far too busy rocking out. My heart started leaping. I don't know why I was nervous. I'd been with girls before. Maybe because it had always happened so easy in the past. I barely had to do anything. Beth jumped me in her own bed. The girl before that gave herself to me with no hesitation. All I had to do was be present. It was a little different with Vicki. We would go through the whole courting ritual. We spent a few weeks getting to know each other. We brushed hands or arms a few times but that was all.

This was the night that it would all come into play.

Next, I had to get rid of Scotty.

I gave plenty of hints that fell on deaf or stubborn ears.

I must've spent close to an hour dropping hints. Eventually I think he just got bored because he suddenly stood up and left. 'I'm going home. This is boring.'

I thought of doing the whole "fake" asking them to stay thing—'Oh really, you want to go?' or 'You're not leaving are you?' or 'All ready?' I decided to say nothing and watched him jump out of the window.

That was my queue.

Vicki had let me fondle with her hand for the past hour. I think I touched every single inch of it a thousand times. And then she said the words that prompted that "real" asking them to stay thing—'Oh, don't go' or 'Don't leave yet' or 'all ready?'

I think she was testing me because after only three quick protests she agreed to stay a bit longer.

'Why don't you come up on the bed with me then? It is yours after all'.

That's all the invitation I needed. Quick smart I jumped from the floor and slid in beside Vicki.

Our heads shared the pillow. Our bodies fought over mattress space.

Every inch closer I got to Vicki she moved twice as close.

We were embraced and kissing before I even realised. Most of that probably had to do with the fact that I was stoned. Let's just say that the room was spinning and it wasn't particularly from love.

Our kiss lasted for the whole Appetite for Destruction album. I hadn't ventured further. That changed when the 5 cd system skipped to the next album and Girls, Girls, Girls kicked in.

It was the soundtrack to our first night together. No Celine Dion, Boys to Men and Elton John. Hell no! It was Guns N' Roses, Motley Crue and Metallica.

As the first riff blazed away I went for glory. I was lying on top of her, propped up on one arm. My hand grazed right over her breast and down her tummy. I was going for the prize. When I got to the top of her shorts I undid the button and unzipped.

She didn't flinch a bit. She kissed me harder in anticipation.

The only obstacle between my eager hand and her love patch was a pair of cotton white undies. I grabbed the top of them and pulled towards our feet. They came down easily. It was made even easier when Vicki lifted her body so that I could slide her undies and pants down the length of her legs. She was naked from the waist down. My hand slid back up her leg and I inserted a finger.

She winced and pulled me closer.

Within a few strokes she was moist. My finger was hitting the mark.

Vicki was squirming and undoing my shorts at the same time. I took a brief reprieve from her pubic mound and took my pants off.

I was as hard and straight as a baseball bat.

Vicki grabbed my bat and started having swinging practise.

This went on for a few minutes before she pushed me back and told me to take the rest of her clothes off.

I obliged.

We were both naked. I was lying on top of her. My chest was pressing against her supple, nicely-sized breasts.

We made eye contact and held it whilst she guided me inside of her.

We mustn't have got past three thrusts when Scotty came climbing back through the window.

'Fuck off!' I urged him to leave.

Scotty lingered for a moment and climbed back out the window.

I don't know why he lingered. All there was to see was my bare arse.

Vicki didn't even notice. She kept at it, grabbing my hips and pulling my groin towards hers.

I was deep inside Vicki, we were panting and sweating profusely.

And then Mum walked in.

'Oh my', she started 'I'm so sorry'.

'Mum, please!'

Vicki noticed this time.

She hid her head under my arm and we stopped rocking.

'I'm sorry'.

Mum left.

Vicki looked up at me with a smirk, grabbed my shoulders and rolled us over. She was now on top of me. She sat up straight, put her hands on my tummy and started to slowly gyrate her hips. That set me off. Within 3 minutes she was slumped over my spent body.

We fell asleep in each other's arms that night. Naked, in lust and stoned.

When I woke up, Vicki was gone.

I got dressed and went out to the kitchen where I found Mum, Nathan and Suzie sitting at the table having breakfast. There was a spread of bacon and eggs on a big plate in the middle of the table. Around that sat three plates full of food that they ate off. There were two spare plates on the table. I guessed one was for me but the second I had no idea.

Then I got my answer.

I heard the toilet flush. A tap was turned on then off and the bathroom door opened.

Vicki walked out, dressed in a pair of my shorts and her top and kissed me on the cheek as she walked past me. 'Morning'. She took the seat beside Suzie.

Suzie smiled at me and offered the same greeting.

Mum and Nathan looked at me. They were both grinning too.

I shook my head, offered my reply 'Morning' and took my seat at the table.

Mum started the conversation. 'So Vicki, how long have you known my son'.

'Long enough to be having this conversation with you over breakfast'.

Nice answer Vicki.

Nathan chuckled.

Mum nodded her head. 'I suppose so'.

All three of them hit Vicki with an avalanche of questions over breakfast. To her credit she had an answer for every one of them.

I could tell that she was winning over three new fans because by the time Vicki went home that day she hugged every one of them. They hugged her in return and suggested she return any time.

Vicki took them up on that offer. She was over my house morning, noon and night. They only time she wasn't there was when I was at work. Even then she'd visit the other three.

This pissed Scotty off to no end.

There was no way Mum would let Scotty over if I wasn't home and he'd lived next door for 11 years. Here's this girl that has only been on the scene for a matter of months and Mum was more than happy to facilitate a visit from her any time I wasn't around.

I guess it was inevitable that Vicki and Suzie would become close. They spent a lot of time together. There was a lot of year's difference in age but I guess that doesn't matter. Girls stick together.

I think Suzie looked up to Vicki as a big sister. That made me feel good.

As long as Suzie never found out what we did behind closed doors.

We would get blazed on some harsh drugs, rip each other's clothes off and treat our bodies like leggo blocks—discovering what parts fit into where.

Mum knew half of it. She was aware that we were having sex. But she didn't know what came before it. And generally after.

Instead of the whole cigarette after sex thing, we would lie in bed naked and suck back on a dirty bong.

The room always smelt of marijuana and sex. We started hiding the stench with scented candles. Mum didn't think anything of it. She just thought that it was a little touch of Vicki's. A feminine touch.

I didn't tell her otherwise. It was hiding our little secret after all.

It wasn't a secret for long but.

CHAPTER 18

Moving Out

One night Scotty and Vicki were both over when our safe and cozy world was rocked to its core.

We had all put in and brought a quarter of an ounce of fine grass. That's a nice amount for three people to sit back and get stoned all weekend on but we only got through part of Friday night.

Vicki was always first to have a smoke. Ladies first. She put all she had into it, pulled back hard and was now sitting there basking in the head spin. What a set of lungs. Scotty went after her and was in a similar state. He was giggling about something. I can't remember what. Probably nothing. Maybe himself.

Vicki got to giggling also.

I felt left out so I quickly packed the cone so I could find out what was so funny.

I was part way through pulling back on the bong when Mum walked in with Suzie.

'Vicki, Suzie wants to show you what she made—'.

Mum's look was one I would never forget. Here was her son with his mouth attached to an ugly, dirty, disgusting old plastic bottle with a piece of hose sticking out, dirty black water in the bottom and a tiny bon fire in the hose.

I'll never forget that look. It was a look of utter disappointment.

Suzie didn't comprehend what was happening. She looked at Vicki and Scotty laughing hysterically as I hid the bong behind my back.

Smoke was lingering in the air above our heads.

Suzie coughed. 'What's that smell Mum?'

'Nothing love. Come on, let's go show Nathan again'.

Mum turned Suzie around and led her out the door. She returned half a minute later and closed the door behind her. I could tell she was furious as she spoke to me and my red-eyed friend and girlfriend.

'What the hell are you doing? How dare you bring that stuff into my house? And while your sister is in the next room'.

Scotty was silent.

Vicki was quietly spoken. 'We're so sorry. We never thought Suzie would see it'.

'What, you think you could go on and do this every day without the chance that one of those times she may walk in un-announced?.

'I know. We're really sorry'.

Mum asked me what I had to say for myself.

'Sorry Mum'.

'That's it? You know, Nathan tried to tell me that this was happening but I didn't believe him. Maybe I just didn't want to'. Mum looked at Scotty. 'Does your Mum know that you do this?'

'Yes', Scotty started 'She just told me to not bring it into her house'.

'So you thought you'd bring it into mine instead?!'

Scotty's points with Mum were rapidly diminishing. And he barely had any to gamble with.

He didn't reply. I did.

'Mum, it was my idea. Not Vicki's. Not Scotty's.

'That's even worse'.

'I know. Sorry'.

'Stop saying that'.

The smoke had faded and the room was clearing. Mum's temper was a different matter.

'If you want to do that crap go get your own place'.

And that's all it took. I did just that.

Within a week Vicki and I had moved out together. Dallas had told us that his cousin lived in this big two story place that he was thinking of moving into. Apparently there was room enough for all of us. Vicki and I could live downstairs while Dallas and his cousin, Pete, would live upstairs.

The bottom level was self contained. It had all we needed to live—Bedroom, Kitchen with stove and fridge, bathroom with a shower and a toilet. We wouldn't even need to venture upstairs.

It was sad to leave Mum and Suzie. They both cried but I assured them that I'd visit all the time.

I had no money to move and lacked most necessities but Grace helped me there.

Even though I rarely saw her, when I did she was always so gracious and helpful. Grace fronted the bond money and helped us furnish the place. It was modest furniture but it was furniture none the less.

How do these things happen? I went from being an accomplice to adultery and schlepping off my Mother to having a steady girlfriend, working a full time job and living out of home.

Was I finally growing up?

No.

It was clearly evident that our house would be a house of drugs. All of the tenants smoked drugs.

Dallas and Pete did some heavier stuff. Mostly speed and acid.

It wasn't long before I sampled my first taste of Speed. This was one of those times I told you about earlier.

We were set to go to a Music Festival. I had intended to take some grass with me. I'd carry a pipe with me to smoke it in. You could get small quantities of pot into the grounds where the festival was held. And if you were sneaky, a pipe was an easy thing to get through security.

I'd pull the pipe into three parts and place these in different parts of my clothes.

The cone would be tucked into the brim of my hat. The mouth piece was stuffed into my wallet and the pipe was jammed into my sock.

As soon as we were through the gate I'd assemble the instrument and get high.

I'd normally stuff the bag of grass down my undies since security never patted you down there. They only checked pockets which was the last place you'd try to sneak pot in.

Before this particular festival Dallas and Pete were raving about the advantages of doing some speed before the festival.

'Man, take a hit of speed and you'll be buzzing all day. You wouldn't need to take any shit with you.'

Dallas sold it well.

'It'll fuck you up and you'll think every bit of music you hear is a gift from Satan'.

Pete's pitch was better.

Vicki and I both took some.

Vicki had done it before so she got mine ready for me, which was rather simple.

We got a bottle of water, filled up the lid with some of that water, poured the white crystal powder into that same water, stirred it good and then drunk it. You'd fill the lid again and drink the water to ensure you got all the speed. That was all there was to it.

It crept up slowly but eventually I was flying on a totally different cloud.

It's hard to describe to someone what it feels like to be on speed if they've never done it. In short it just gives you energy to burn. Everything you do is done with the most enthusiasm you have ever felt and everything you do suddenly feels like the best fucking thing to do at the time.

I was blitzing before we even left for the festival.

Vicki, me, Pete, Dallas and a few of his friends went.

I still ended up taking some pot with me. Just in case. A few joints.

Little did I know how long the effects of speed would last.

I was buzzing all festival, that whole night and the next day. Vicki and I had just about the greatest love-making session that night.

I wasn't compelled to take more but. One quick taste did me.

After the weekend of the festival I was back on the marijuana. That did the job for me so there was no need to go onto anything harder.

I nearly forgot something that happened at the Festival. I want to tell you about it because it was the funniest thing I had ever seen or heard.

It might still be the funniest thing I have ever witnessed.

We were that high and eager to get to the festival and let our minds be taken to places unknown, we were inside the grounds when the first band of the day was into their set.

The first bands at a big festival are always unknown, up-and-coming bands. They are usually local bands on the rise.

At this festival the first band was kicking-arse.

We walked into a wall of sound that made my heart jump from my skin.

I lost control and couldn't stop jumping around.

We checked the program for the band name but all it said was 'Local band'.

Whoever they were, they rocked the shit out of the small crowd that was slowly expanding. The band was certainly making new fans this day.

All of a sudden we noticed two young girls running through the crowd throwing pieces of paper above their head. One of these pieces of paper landed at Dallas' feet. He picked it up and produced the biggest smile.

I hadn't seen what was written on the paper when Dallas held the piece of paper above his head and started shouting 'I've won! I've won the Skunk Lotto!'

Dallas thought he had won some marijuana jackpot.

I found one of the pieces of paper, picked it up and read it: SUNK LOTO.

The band was called Sunk Loto.

Dallas swears to this day that his sticker read SKUNK LOTTO. He thought he'd hit it lucky.

'I've won the Skunk Lotto!'

Hilarious!

That band grew to become one of my favourite bands of all time. Home grown anyway.

I was shattered when they split up almost 10 years, one EP and two albums later.

The singer and drummer have gone on to form a new band that I have high expectations for.

Time will tell.

So my first foray into Speed was a great experience.

I did it a few more times. Most of those were for another festival.

There wer so many drugs going through our house. Upstairs, Dallas and Pete would be hitting the hard stuff and doing cones in between.

Downstairs, Vicki and I would be pulling back bongs like they were becoming extinct.

Spending as much money as we all were on our habits, it was only inevitable that something had to give.

There was a plan for this but.

Pete knew a guy.

Here's how bills got paid in our household.

Before I go on I have to tell you—Pete was gay. He was openly gay and never tried to hide it.

This never bothered me. He knew I was with Vicki. A girl.

(Listen to me, going on as if, just because I was a guy, Pete was attracted to me. I don't think he ever was. He never made a move on me I'll say that much).

Pete would pay the bigger bills when they came in. And how he got the money wasn't revealed to me until years later, long after we had moved out, when I ran into Dallas.

Here was his play.

There was apparently some guy that Pete used to refer to as his Uncle. Pete said that he was in the money and was always happy to help with bills when we were struggling, which was most of the time.

So anytime a big bill came in Pete would be all 'I'm off to see Uncle John (Not his real name). He'll help us out. I'll pay this bill'.

Suited us. I always wondered what it'd be like to have a rich Uncle that could get me out of binds.

Turned out that Pete didn't know what it was like either.

This "Uncle" turned out to be anything but.

In Dallas' words "Pete screwed some married guy and now bribes him with it. He tells this guy that he'll tell his wife all about their night together if he doesn't give him money.

Pete would go down to where this man worked, where he was struggling to make ends meet. Where his fellow workers respected him, and threaten to bring it all crashing down around him.

What was this guy meant to do? He indulged in one night of curious desire and now he'll pay for it for the rest of his life. Or at least the rest of Pete's.

Of course, the guy could come clean to his wife but who'd want to do that?

I'd pay up.

And so did Pete's poor victim.

My life with Vicki in our downstairs love nest was going great.

I'd wake up, share a wonderful breakfast with Vicki and we'd both head off to work.

Vicki was an office worker for some storage place.

When we got home we'd sit and talk over a hot dinner, do the dishes, clean ourselves up and head straight for the bong.

We were stuck in that routine.

Every night we were both still going to bed stoned.

We had learnt that there were free drugs to be had if we went upstairs and sat with Pete while he watched TV.

Pete always, I mean always, had a freshly chopped bowl of pot. It was a white cereal bowl. It had been used so many times that the bottom of the bowl was stained green.

On the days where we couldn't afford a stick between us, Vicki and I would go sit with Pete and in less than 5 minutes we'd be sharing a bong with him.

We'd get stoned and then leave him to watch his shows. He never cared and also didn't catch on that we'd sit with him long enough to get stoned and then we were gone, back to our own drug den.

We'd hope the drugs were good enough to last until bed time.

As much as our home lives revolved around drugs, I made sure to visit Mum as often as I could.

I'd also take the time to stop and check in on Grace. Her health was declining as the years went on but I still knew I could find her out in the garden every day between 4 and 5.

One day, out of the blue, Mum called me and asked if I could head straight over to see her. Luckily it was on a day when we had no drugs, no money to buy drugs and, thankfully, Pete wasn't home.

I was able to be straight when I sent to see her.

I said out of the blue before because it wasn't often that Mum called me.

I thought there must be some real big reason for her to call and ask me to go straight over.

I had no idea just how big it'd be.

CHAPTER 19
. . . .

Redemption

I must've been dressed and out front of Mums in under ten minutes. And considering there was a 20 minute drive between our places I think I did pretty well.

I didn't even notice the car sitting in the driveway. A car I had never seen before.

I ascended the front stairs where I was greeted by Suzie. She was Seven years old now and growing taller daily.

The first three words she said as she hugged me should've told me all I needed to know about my reason for being there.

'You're Dad's here.'

I wondered why she didn't say "Our", "Our dad's here".

Mum hushed Suzie into the house and hugged me.

'Someone's here to see you son.'

I looked down at her. 'He's here?'

I still thought the man who had posed as my Dad for all those years was waiting to see me.

Why would he come back and why would Mum call me to come see him? He wasn't even my *real* Dad.

That's when it occurred to me. If Suzie was saying that my Dad was here to see me and it wasn't the guy who taught me that same lesson over and over, that could only mean one thing.

Mum took my hand and led me into the front lounge room. Nathan and Suzie were sitting on the three-seater. When I walked in Nathan took Suzie's hand and went to stand up. 'Come on Suzie Love. Let's go play in your room.'

Mum nodded her head toward them to signal that she agreed that would be a good idea.

'No', I started 'stay'.

Mum nodded again and they both sat down.

Sitting in one of the single-seaters was a man I had never seen before. He looked to be about 50 years old. Give or take. It was hard to get a good gauge of his age due to the scruffy beard that covered his face. He was a little potty in the stomach and was a little short (just below average I'd say).

It occurred to me that the guy looked a bit like me when I let a three day growth stretch out to a few weeks.

Oh my god!

The thought hit me like an anvil in the side of my head.

This was my *real* Dad. The man who, along with my mother, conceived me.

Shit! I was looking at my *real* Dad.

The resemblance grew with every second.

I have always though from that day on that my Dad reminds me of Jeff Bridges. You know the actor who played "The Dude" in The Big Lebowski. Everyone knows Jeff Bridges. He's just about the finest actor of our or any generation. I say just about because Johnny Depp may throw his name into the mix. I think Jeff Bridges edges him out though.

If you haven't seen the following Jeff Bridges movies, do yourself a favour and find them:

- The Big Lebowski
- True Grit
- The Moguls
- Crazy Heart (The Academy can't be wrong, right?)

An incredible actor.

If my Dad looks like Jeff Bridges I wonder if I will when I'm older?

The strange man in the small chair stood up and stretched his arm in my direction. 'Hello son'.

I didn't know what to do. How do you react to that? Was he acknowledging me the way a father refers to his child or was he just calling me son like older man seem to always do to younger ones? Either way, I had no idea how to react.

I looked at Mum. She held her hand over her mouth and had a tear in her eyes.

I shook his hand. He had a very firm handshake.

Years later, when our relationship had bloomed, my Dad gave me the greatest piece of advice I had ever received. And now I want to pass it on to you.

'Son', he said 'you can tell all you need to know about a Man by the way he shakes your hand. If he's a confident man his shake will be firm. If he is shy and not so sure of himself his shake will be loose. He'll barely put any pressure on your hand. You know a man's character the moment you share a handshake'.

And I must say that every time I have ever shaken a hand I knew immediately what kind of person I was dealing with. And was rarely wrong.

The fact that Dad's handshake was the firmest I have ever encountered was testament to the advice.

'Hello', I replied.

There was silence that would've lasted forever if it wasn't for Mum. Bless her.

'Can I get you men a drink?'

'Please'.

'What would you like Henry?'

Henry. That was his name. It suited him.

'Just a coffee, please'.

'Sure. Nathan can you help me please? Bring Suzie'.

'But I don't want to', Suzie protested.

Nathan knew exactly what to do. He had a way with Suzie. For not having any kids of his own he certainly knew how to deal with them.

'Come on Suze. I'll let you make a chocolate shake'.

And with that she was gone.

Dad Henry stood up as Mum was exiting the room. 'Do you mind if I bring Carol in? She's waiting out in the car'.

Carol? I had a Step-Mother.

Mum turned while Nathan and Suzie made for the kitchen. 'You mean she's been out there the whole time?'

'I didn't know if it'd be appropriate to have her here'.

'Of course it'd be ok', Mum protested 'Go and get her'.

I was left stranded alone in the lounge room while everyone attended to their tasks.

Henry and Carol came through the front door. I was introduced and took the opportunity to ask Carol to take a seat.

They sat down and held hands.

Mum returned with the drinks and we all chatted well into the night. It didn't take long before Suzie gave in to the temptation of the Golden Slumber. That left the adults to converse.

I found out that Mum and Dad had split up when I was eight months old just like she had said. Mum had left dad. It devastated him and took a long time for him to recover. This recovery was eventually made easier when he met Carol. They hit it off straight away and have been inseparable ever since.

I had to dig a bit to find out the reason my parents separated but it was revealed.

Dad was in the Air Force. During the late 60's and early 70's he served three stints in The Vietnam War. Like a lot of young men at that time, this meant being away from your family. In between his 1st and 2nd stint Mum fell pregnant with me. Dad was away the whole time my Mum was pregnant. He missed the birth and didn't get to see me until I was 5 months old. As much as the baby—me—should've been bringing them closer together, the fact that they were a world apart didn't do them any favours. Mum said that by the time Dad came home their relationship had been broken by the time apart. Mum had been pregnant alone, she gave birth alone, raised me alone and, upon Dad's return, found it better to stay alone.

3 months into Dad's return they were separated.

So I only ever lived with my real Dad for 3 months.

Mum's told me over the years to not blame him, and I don't.

Sitting in that room with my real Dad and Step-Mum was certainly a surreal experience. The similarities in our features were amazing. We both had the same prominent eyebrows. I don't mean hairy brows, no, the skull around our eyes, at the top (behind the brow) was very evident. We both had larger ears. Not sticking-out-type ears, ours were big but close to the head. Dad had a receding hair line and you could tell even in my early 20's that I was destined for the same fate.

But as I said, he reminded me of Jeff Bridges so I was ok with how the 50 year old me was going to look.

Dad had lived all around our country. That's why he never came around or tried to contact me earlier. He and Carol had finally decided to settle down and they were going to do that about 100 kilometres from where I grew up. They never had any children of their own. I don't know if I could've handled step-siblings as well. The shock of Dad showing up was enough.

And then he asked me something that threw me off at first but I quickly warmed to the idea.

'Yes, we're setting up camp close so', he looked at me directly 'if it's ok with you, I'd like to see you some more.

'Of course', I replied. I loved the idea. What've I got to lose right?

I'm glad I made that decision. It has brought me nothing but joy.

My Dad is a wonderful, fantastic man. I found out that he loved all the old Rock and Roll that I lived for. We certainly bonded over our talks about music.

He was a man of ethics, integrity and honour. He spoke with a polite, quite manner and his speech was perfectly presented. Pardons and Thank you were top of his vocabulary list. Carol and my Dad lived a modest but very fulfilling life. They weren't rich, far from it but Dad had been smart enough throughout his life to know that he'd need things later not now. He spent wisely, saved even better and had wonderful guidance in regards to investment.

I think his discipline came from his years in the Force.

Dad's arrival had left me a little torn though. By this time I had grown close to Nathan also. As with my Dad, I shared many a word with him about music. I didn't want to desert Nathan just because someone else had come along. Even if it was my dad.

Nathan went so far as to mention it one day, not long after my Dad first showed up.

'You know, it's ok if you'd rather see your Dad then hang out with me'.

'What do you mean? I like hanging out with you'.

'I know you do but he is your Dad, you should give him a chance'.

'I am. We see each other often enough'.

'I hope you do. He's taken a big step to get back into your life'.

'I know'.

'Ok then. Just know that I won't be offended if you ever want to hang out with him instead of me'.

'I know. Thanks Nathan'.

'No worries'.

So I went from having no Dad but being too young to know, to having an imposter ruin my childhood with his lessons that I shall never forget, to having no father figure in my life, to having a stranger take me in like his own, then my real Dad enters the picture and I have two father figures. Both I would do anything for.

Life is a funny thing.

By the time Dad and Carol had left that first night we had already planned a second. I told them all about Vicki and they insisted I bring her along. We organised a dinner at some restaurant in town for the following week.

I went home and told Vicki all about it; how much we looked alike, the fact that I had a Step-Mother and that they only lived an hour's drive away. I spent hours talking to her about him. I couldn't stop babbling. Vicki couldn't get a word in edge wise.

All of this happened after I had a few hits from my Bong, of course.

Vicki was hovering on the walls when I walked in the door. I had to catch up.

I never told Dad about my drug habit and he never found out. So if you're reading this Dad, I'm sorry. It's not something that you want to be common knowledge.

Spoiler Alert

I kicked the habit a few years after I met Dad. My drug taking years are well behind me.

I promise.

But for the time being, back when I was getting through my early 20's I was absolutely, definitely, totally, miserably and hopelessly dependant of Marijuana.

I like to think I hid it well.

If you ever knew Dad, Thank you for not confronting me. I would've been crushed.

I woke up the next morning, I took to calling this my "Post *real* Dad" era, and went straight over to see Grace. I had to tell her the news.

'Really?' she started with a huge smile 'I'm so happy for you love'.

'Thank you Grace'.

'So tell me about him'.

We sat on the front porch watching cars drive by and drunk our tea.

'Well, um. What do you want to know?'

'Everything dear. Please tell me everything'.

I sipped on my hot tea 'Ok, well he looks just like Jeff Bridges'.

'Who's that dear?'

Obvious response.

'No one. I look just like him'.

'Well of course you do. You are his offspring. His Spawn. A younger version of him'.

I never thought of that. I think I was far from being a copy, a version of my Dad. Not unless Dad was taught sick lessons when he was young, got into trouble for stupid shit and took drugs everyday for over five years.

I'd highly doubt it, all though he was a teenager through the 60's and 70's.

I think Grace meant in looks only. In that case I agree.

'Right', I started 'and he loves music as much as I do. He went to War'.

I always had a fascination about war. I'd dedicated my learning to World War 2 but all of a sudden I took a bigger interest in The Vietnam War. After all, I now knew someone who had experienced it. Why I never asked my dad about it I don't know, but I didn't. I guess I'd read enough stories about veterans to know that veterans didn't usually like to talk about their experiences.

I'm going to ask you one day Dad.

'Did he?'

I knew grace would appreciate that. She'd told me many times how her husband had been in the Second World War. She loved telling me about how they met when he was stationed a town away from her home when she was only a teen. 'He could've had the pick of any girl in our town, with his charming uniform, but he chose me', Grace would state with a sense of achievement.

'He did. He served 3 tours of Vietnam'.

'A terrible war'.

'Was it?' I knew nothing about it back then. I was stubborn to the harsh realities of such a bitter time in our nation's existence. Now that I know about it I can agree that it was a war, like all others that was fought for the wrong reasons and should never have been fought at all.

'Oh yes Dear, horrible'.

And it was horrible. I have read about it in recent times and can't believe the words that jump off the pages. The way the Vietnamese treated Prisoners of War. There was no Geneva convention-type treatment. If you were a POW you were dead. Then you had the whole Agent Orange Operation. How a country can use a substance that could affect their own troops in the hope it'd disable the enemy I'll never know. My Dad has health issues to this day because of that "Crop Spray".

'But tell me about your Dad'.

So I did.

I spent the next hour telling her every little detail I had learnt so far about the Man that spawned me. And she listened happily. Grace was a great listener. When she needed to she came up with responses or advice that were sheer words of wisdom.

I was only learning about what it was like to have my real Dad around when a bombshell was dropped that quickly showed me the other side of that experience.

CHAPTER 20

Joy (of Parenthood)

Life is a funny thing isn't it? I said earlier that I didn't believe in God, and Fate and Destiny and all that sort of thing. But here's the scenario: Out of my 20 years on this green and blue planet I had lived 14 of that with a Man who I thought was my Dad only to find out he was an impostor. For the proceeding few years there was no father figure for me, only Mum. And that was enough. Then Nathan came along and, all though he and Mum hadn't married at this time, I looked up to him because he was a great guy, nice to Mum and Suzie and, most importantly, treated my Mother like she was a Princess. And one day a man shows up and declares himself as my real Dad. This was still sinking in when Vicki came home one day with a declaration of her own.

I was upstairs eagerly helping Pete smoke away his stash of prime grass. My mouth was attached to the bong as Vicki walked up the stairs.

Whenever she got home from work and couldn't find me downstairs she knew exactly where I was.

She walked in and stood at the doorway.

"Hey. Want one?'

It wasn't my stuff but I wasn't shy about offering it away.

'No. Can we go downstairs?'

Pete said hi to Vicki. She responded in the same vein.

I looked at her, then to Pete who I offered a shrug and turned back to Vicki.

'One more cone and I'll come down'.

Vicki turned around, slammed the door behind her and stomped down the stairs.

Pete had a puzzling look on offer.

'Beats me', I added.

I took in the smoke, exhaled, handed Pete the bong and started for the stairs. I turned back and thanked him for the drugs, not knowing that I had just pulled back on my last hit.

When I got downstairs Vicki was sitting on the bed. She patted the bed signalling for me to join her. It was an unusual situation: we were in the room on our bed and only one of us was stoned. This *never* happened. We were either both happily smashed out of our minds or both strung out, sober and miserably trying to score.

Vicki didn't think any less of me for being stoned while she wasn't.

It didn't occur to me think about why she had rejected the bong. I didn't have to think because the first thing Vicki said when I sat down made it quite clear.

'I'm pregnant'.

I was floored.

My head was already spinning as it was. I thought "Me a dad?" right after my first thought which was along the lines of "What was that shit Pete gave me? I'm hammered".

I had to reply though because it was clear Vicki was waiting.

If you remember when I told you about the time Suzie was born, you'll be able to guess what I said.

'Oh that's fantastic! I'm so happy for you. You're going to be an excellent Mother'.

Remember: the only correct response to the statement 'I'm pregnant'. Well I started with that.

And it was wrong.

'You're happy for *me*? What the fuck?!'

Whoops. One word brought me unstuck. Back peddle! Back peddle!

'Us, I mean I'm happy for us'.

'Then say *us*, not *you*',

'Right, right. I'm happy for us. But you are going to be a great Mother'.

'It's not all about me'.

'Right'.

'You have no idea, do you?'

'Wha-'

'You're happy for me. I'll be a good Mother?'

'Yeah, that's right'.

'Idiot'.

Vicki hopped off the bed and went out to the kitchen area.

I followed, head spinning and all.

'Vicki, what's wrong?'

I had no idea the moody attitude kicked in so early. What else could it be right?

'*Us*. How about us? You're happy for *us*. *We'll* be great parents'.

'Sure. Of course we will be. I am happy for us'.

'Then say it'.

'I just did. Sorry babe. I'm just a little stoned. That stuff Pete's got . . . wow'.

Vicki leant against the sink while I grabbed a can of drink from the fridge. I kissed her and guzzled down the soft drink.

'Well we need to talk about that'.

'About what? It's a can. You told me not to drink out of the bottle. This is a can'.

'Not that, you idiot. Drugs. All this pot'.

'What about it? Pete's got heaps. Go up there I'm sure he'll give you all you want'.

'Don't you get it?'

'Get what?'

This wasn't one of my finer moments, I'll admit.

'I'm pregnant. I can't be putting that shit into my body. I am going to have a life forming in there'.

I didn't like where this was heading. 'Right'.

'I won't be doing that stuff anymore'.

I threw the empty can into the bin.

'You're just going to give up? Just like that?'

'No—'.

I knew it.

'—*we're* going to give up'.

'What!?'

'You can't expect me to do this alone. I can't give up and have you doing it around me all the time'.

So that's what this was about. She didn't want to be tempted so I had to give up in order to eliminate that possibility.

'And I don't want the baby to be around that environment. I can't be having you blowing smoke everywhere just so I can inhale it and harm our baby'.

Oh, right. That.

'I didn't think of that'.

And I hadn't. Not until she said it.

'Yes well. Things have to change'.

And this is where things got a little soppy.

'We're going to have a baby. There's going to be a life inside of me. A life that *we* put there. We created. We're going to be parents'.

I thought it best to match Vicki's enthusiasm.

'We are aren't we? This is fantastic!'

Vicki cuddled up to me and nudged her head under my chin.

'It's wonderful . . . Daddy'.

Daddy? Me? Daddy! I didn't know if I was ready for that. Who am I kidding, of course I wasn't. I was still a young guy who liked getting stoned, spending all my money (whatever was left after I brought my drugs) on new CD's and clothes. Now I'd have some little mouth that was going to be dependent on me for at least the next 16 years.

Don't misread what I'm telling you, I was excited. I was more than excited. I was over the moon. But I was also shit-scared. I've since found out that it's normal, it's expected for the father to be scared. Every little detail about this new thing in my life scared me more then I'd ever been before.

Not Vicki though. At least she never said so.

She went into it all guns blazing. She read every book about parenting known to man. She even marked pages for me to look over. I wasn't a reader back then though so it was quite an effort for me to read what she wanted me to learn. But I did.

My first day as an expecting Dad was no different than the one before except that I went to bed stone cold sober. I'd promised Vicki that I would not do any drugs while she was around and I intended to stick to it. But damn it was tough. I went from being stoned senseless every day to being as straight as a pencil. For the first month at least I couldn't get to sleep. Every night I would lay in bed and listen to Vicki quietly breathe while she visited the land of bounding sheep and happy dreams. Me, I was scratching the ceiling. My body had got use to falling asleep stoned. It hadn't known any different for some time. This was going to be tough, that was obvious.

I was tempted almost every day to break my promise. I'd walk upstairs and see Dallas and Pete settling in for a big session. The aroma crept up my nostrils and seemed to be absorbed by my pores. I wanted to get stoned. I so badly needed to. But I didn't. It didn't stop them from offering but. Bastards!

We chose to wait a few weeks before we told our families. This was so that we could get a Doctor's confirmation that Vicki was definitely pregnant. The Doctor confirmed and with this in our hand we went to break the news to Vicki's Mum. She was happy for us but it wasn't a big thing. You see, Vicki had two older sisters who had already had kids so her Mum was a Grandmother several times over. So while she was happy for us, it wasn't anything new to her. The two older sisters were over the moon about it. Their little sister had finally got pregnant. She was one of them.

The next step was telling Mum. Vicki and I went over and had dinner with her, Nathan and Suzie. It wasn't commonplace for me to suggest we have dinner together so Mum knew there was a reason behind it, more so then just a "dinner". She didn't let on though. It was general chit chat; How's work? How's the house? Suzie, how are you doing at School? The alarms came on when Vicki rejected a glass of alcohol.

'Oh no, thank you. Not for me.'

Mum bit. 'Why not dear? You don't have to drive. It's only one drink'.

'Mum, its ok. She doesn't feel like one'. I stated in Vicki's defence.

Vicki was clearly nervous. 'I can't'.

Everything fell silent. It was Suzie who broke it.

'Why can't you Vicki?'

Mum tried back-peddling. 'Suz, honey, let's leave it'.

'No, I'm sorry', Vicki started whilst she took a hold of my hand that was resting on the table 'we have something to tell you'.

Mum shrugged at Nathan. Nathan shrugged back. They both looked at me.

'What is it dear?'

Vicki took up the question.

'I'm pregnant'.

My Mum's eyes welled up immediately. It was like a tap behind her eyes had been switched on and off so quick that the water only sat at the end of the hose.

'Are you sure dear?' She looked to me as if my answer would hold more credence. 'Is this true?'

'Yes'. Vicki and I answered in unison.

Mum looked back to Nathan. He smiled. She stood up and came around to our side of the table. Vicki stood up and greeted her. Nathan leaned over the table and offered his extended hand in congratulations.

'Congratulations pal'.

'Thank you', I said as I received and returned his firm handshake.

Mum and Vicki's hug lingered long enough for Suzie to jump from her seat and wrap her small arms around what she could of the both of them. When they eventually let go Mum took me in her arms and held me close.

She whispered something in my ear that I think I'm going to keep to myself.

Before she had a chance to let go properly Suzie had jumped up on a seat and launched for my torso. I managed to catch her. She squeezed me tighter than anyone that night.

'I can't believe it. I'm an aunty'.

This hadn't even occurred to me. I'd made Suzie an aunty at only 8 years old.

'Yeah, I guess you will be'.

We all sat back down and went through our plans for the next 9 months. And I gotta tell you, they flew by quicker than the time Mum was pregnant with Little Suzie. After that night at Mums we went straight over to Grace's the next day and told her. Well, you should've seen her reaction.

"Oh my Lord! That's tremendous dear. When is it due? Have you two got everything you need dear?'

"We'll get everything'.

'Well whatever you need help with you let me know'.

"We will Grace'.

What is it with old people and babies? I think it's the whole end of the scale thing where they're at or nearing the end of their life and they hold something in their arms that has only just begun theirs. An old person is always so mesmerised by something that is so young and fresh and new.

That's my opinion. But it's true right? Old people love babies. Test my theory if you doubt it. If you have a baby, or know someone who does, get them to walk into a room full of people of mixed ages. I guarantee old ladies will have drool dripping from their dentures at the prospect of holding the little bundle of new life. And the younger people, well they'll be off trying to persuade a stranger to go home with them in the hope of not producing something new for the old ladies to drool over.

It was a similar situation when I told Dad and Carol so I don't think I need to go into detail. Let me just say that Dad was crying before Carol shed a tear. He loved the idea of being a Grandfather. As far as he was concerned he only just started to be a Dad. I agreed. Nothing against him, that's just how it turned out.

The one person I didn't tell was Scotty. He had found himself a girl that was willing to put up with his stupid, dare-this, dare-that lifestyle. I don't remember her name but I do remember that because of her I saw Scotty less. I think I was ok with that. Not sure. My relationship with him was always a hard thing to define. For as long as I'd known him he was daring me to do stupid stuff. He was a bastard to almost everyone we knew, even me. He had no manners. Was foul-mouthed and didn't care for Vicki.

Yeah, I was ok with that.

He did find out eventually. I'll spare you from that story too.

And then the big day arrived.

It was any other day just like the one previous, and the one before that. I was stacking shelves and helping customers find their precious condiments. A call came over the PA system telling me that I had a call in the office. I went in and picked up line 3.

It was Mum. 'Vicki's gone into labour. We're at the hospital. Hurry up'.

My heart skipped about 5 beats all at once. 'I'm coming'.

I hung up the phone and ran into my boss' office. She knew I was expecting this call at anytime. I didn't have to say a word. She could tell by my actions that it was that time.

'Go', was all she said.

I found it hard to keep to the speed limit heading up to the hospital. I wonder if the Police would let you off of a speeding fine if you told them you're girlfriend was having a baby. Depends on the Cop I guess. I've heard stories.

The Nurse at Reception told me the room Vicki was in—Labour Ward 7. My favourite number is 7 so I immediately took this as a good sign.

The site I ran into was unexpected to say the least. Vicki was pacing the room holding her tummy as if it was about to drop any minute. I guess it was. Mum was sitting in a chair to the side of the bed with her head in her head. Vicki was groaning and mumbling. When I burst through the door her stare pierced my skin.

'Where the fuck have you been!?'

'I had to leave work and drive here through traffic'.

'I don't care what you had to do. You should be here'.

'I am now'.

While this was going on, Mum sat in silence.

'Bout bloody time!' Vicki added.

'Should you be standing up?' I looked at Mum 'Mum, should she be standing up?'

Mum didn't get a response in.

'You try sitting down when you have a sharp-nailed pineapple trying to push itself out of your pea-sized hole'.

'She's right love. Walking around is the best thing. Until she can't handle the pain anymore, she should be on her feet'.

'Thank you. I know what I'm doing'.

The labour lasted 32 hours. Vicki did end up in the bed eventually. The Nurse came in and stuck a big arse needle in her spine. It seemed like Vicki was flying with the pigeons after that. Who needs pot huh? Just go get knocked-up.

When I saw the sharp-nailed pineapple exit the pea-sized hole I nearly gagged. It is quite an experience. I recommend it to anyone. Give it a try.

The moment that baby comes out and makes his or her first noise you realise that it was totally worth it. The nurse slaps its bum and makes it cry to clear the airway, or something, than they wrap the baby in a relevantly-coloured blanket and place it on the Mum's chest. At that moment the Mother/Baby bond is solidified.

Dad's in the room but they can't compete with that bond between the Mother and Baby.

Mum was crying as Vicki held our little bundle. I was perched on the bed beside Vicki who was looking like she had green-out, recovered, drank a carton of beer, greened out again and was now laughing and crying all at the same time. It was beautiful. With my most delicate touch, I was caressing my daughter's head.

I had a Daughter. For the rest of my life I would be some little girls Daddy.

Mum was playing with the babies little fingers. Her tears were dripping right beside the baby, almost landing on her back.

The Nurse broke our trance. 'Do you want to cut the cord, Dad?'

That was the first time I was referred to as Dad. I have to tell you, it was weird.

I looked at Vicki who paid the comment no attention, then to Mum.

'Go on Love'.

I took the scissors from the Nurse and did as she instructed. The cord was cut. The physical connection between Mum and Daughter was broken. I promised myself that that'd be the only time I ever separate them. Or us. (I kept half that promise).

The Nurse cleaned the area and disposed of the cord. 'Do you have a name picked?"

Mum looked at us as if this question hadn't even occurred to her.

I looked at Vicki who was still staring at our baby.

'Vicki?'

No answer.

'We had some names selected but never settled on one, didn't we Vicki'.

No answer.

The baby was asleep on Vicki's tummy. It must be exhausting work for the both of them.

Mum held her hand over her chest. 'Look at that. There's so much Joy in this room'.

Vicki broke out of her trance. 'Joy'.

'That's right love'.

Vicki looked up at me. 'No, Joy, the name. Let's call her Joy'.

I looked at Joy and agreed. 'Joy. I like that'.

Mum has bragged from that day on that she named her first Grandchild. It may have been indirectly but she still said the word first.

Vicki played with Joy's little pink fingers. 'Hello Joy, I'm your Mummy. You're going to be so happy being our Daughter'.

Anything good I have done from that day until now has been done for the Joy in my life.

The Nurse took Joy away to run tests and Vicki slept. Mum and I contacted the family and made arrangement for them all to come and see Joy.

By the end of that afternoon everyone had come by to see the new addition to our family. Dad and Carol stopped in. Nathan brought Suzie up to see her Niece. Vicki's Mum and sister's stopped in, kids in tow. That was hectic. Luckily Vicki had slept well prior to their arrival and was a little livelier. I went and picked Grace up. I tell you, my theory about old people and Babies was even more confirmed on that day. Grace swooped on her like a vulture and didn't let go.

After two days we took Joy home and started our life together as a family.

It didn't take long before our harmony was tested.

CHAPTER 21
. . . .

Strike 2

Now I know it wasn't an ideal situation to bring a newborn baby home to—Living on the lower level of a house where, just a thin floor above there was enough pot to start a plantation, but that was all we had at the time. It was home and it felt like it.

Dallas and Pete had taken to selling. They were dealers. I had never been around more Marijuana in my life and I didn't want any of it. Amazing right? Joy kept me well away from it. We had strangers pulling up in the driveway at all hours of the day. We may as well have put a revolving door in as a gate, there was that much activity. Vicki had made it very clear though that no one was to come down to our part of the house. All the regular buyers knew to go straight to the door upstairs. We had peace and privacy for the better part.

That all fell apart the day we heard loud banging coming from the upstairs entry. Dallas and Pete weren't home (very rare for dealers) so I had to go answer the door before the noise woke Joy. And before Vicki scolded me to death with her frustrated stare.

I tip-toed up the steps and went to the door. As soon as I opened it I was met by no less than 8 Policemen with batons drawn.

They barged straight past me into the living room. I got the feeling they knew exactly what they were looking for and where to find it.

One of the officers pinned me to the ground and held their knee squarely in my back.

'You have the right to remain silent-'

'What's going on? This is a mistake.'

'Anything you say can be held against you-'

'Held against me? You've got the wrong guy'.

The criminal's favourite saying. If criminals had a coat of arms, their motto would be "You've got the wrong guy", and in fine print underneath "I'm innocent".

'Do you live here?"

'Yes, but-'

'Then we've got the right man. We've been monitoring-'

At this point in time Vicki came through the door from downstairs.

'What's going—Oh my God! What're you doing?

One of the Police officers grabbed Vicki and shoved her against the wall. The officer had Vicki's arm bent behind her back.

'Get your fucking hands off her! She hasn't done anything'

'Sir, please, calm down'. The officer looked at Vicki 'Miss, do you live her also?'

'Yes, but we live downstairs. This is a mistake'.

'I told them that'.

'You both live here?'

'Yes, but we-'

'You live at this address?'

'Yes, but there's two other-'

'If you live under this roof you are going to be arrested for being in possession of and dealing Marijuana'.

'But you haven't even found anything'.

And on that queue, on perfect timing, one of the officers exited Pete's room with a garbage bag full of green buds—sticky Marijuana.

'That's not ours!'

'Sir, you are in the house and there are illegal drugs in the house. You're responsible for them'.

Vicki's motherly senses kicked in. Above all the noise she heard Joy crying.

'My baby. Let me go'.

The officer holding Vicki finally got involved. 'There's a baby in the house?'

'Yes, *downstairs*, where me and my boyfriend live'.

The officer holding Vicki looked at who must've been the commanding officer. The CO nodded and the officer let Vicki go.

Vicki looked at me, pinned to the ground by a blue-clothed vigilante.

'Go'.

Vicki bolted down the stairs. An officer followed her.

The officer holding me down lifted me up by the handcuffs that were tightly fastened to my wrists.

'You have to come with us'.

'But I told you, there's two other guys. It's their stuff!'

'Well until we see these other gentlemen we will need to take you into custody'.

'What about Vicki?'

'Officer Parks will deal with her'.

As I was placed in the back of the squad car Vicki came running out with Joy in her arms.

'You can't take him. The stuff isn't even ours. We gave that up'.

Her cries were falling on deaf ears. But she persisted.

'He has a Daughter here to take care of'.

'Take Joy inside Vicki'.

Vicki's cries were being drowned out by Joy's screaming.

I watched through smudged windows as my three week old Daughter hollered with all the might her little lungs could muster. Three week old babies don't remember things, right? I'd hate for Joy to remember that day. Bad enough I have to.

As the squad car reversed out of the driveway, Vicki went back inside the house. She told me after that Joy stopped crying as soon as all the Police and their noise left.

A few minutes later and my first ride in the back of a blue and white car was over.

The Cops left me in handcuffs as they led me through the Police Station and shoved me into a little caged cell. This was my first taste of life behind bars. Why'd I ever go back for seconds?

The cell was small—a mere 3 x 3 metre cage. Within that was a bunk bed that looked as comfortable as a Sao biscuit. There was a tiny toilet in one of the corners that a garden gnome would've been too big for. This would be my home for the next 28 hours.

Every so often I was taken to an interrogation room. Every hour on the hour two big, burly Police Officers led me from the cell to a room that was even smaller. They sat me in a wooden chair that was right in front of a table. One of the Officers sat in the chair opposite and the second paced behind him. There was a single, dim light swinging overhead. I think they must've designed this room based on old Film Noir Cops and Robbers shows. Was I going to get the Good-Cop-Bad-Cop routine?

Apparently not. They were both playing bad.

The guy across from me got right into it.

'What was the stuff for?'

I spoke in a controlled tone. 'It isn't mine. Me and my girlfriend live downstairs.'

'Bullshit!' The Officer added.

I was wrong. They were playing Bad-Cop-Worse-Cop.

The sitting man again. 'There wasn't anyone else there. We have word that you and your partner are the sole tenants at the Address'.

This struck out to me. I looked up into the sitting cops eyes. 'You have word?'

'That's right. We were informed that you and your partner were selling Marijuana out of the house'.

My controlled tone was quickly being lost. 'Someone dobbed us in?'

The pacing cop added more. 'So you admit that you were selling?'

'No, no I didn't say that. I'm just asking if you were there because someone told you that we were selling drugs'.

'I'm not at liberty to go into details'.

'And we wouldn't fucking tell you anyway, scumbag!' Mr. pacing cop spat at me.

'This is bullshit! I—'

'Watch your language Mr.—'

'But it is! My girlfriend and I have a three week old baby in the house. Why would we have illegal drugs there? I wouldn't have my daughter around that shit'.

'Sir. You need to calm your temper down before you get yourself into more trouble'.

'More trouble!' I was furious. 'I shouldn't even be in *this* trouble'.

'But you are' started Mr. pacing cop 'and now you're going to pay for it'.

I slumped back into my chair in a physical display of defeat. My tone suddenly went sullen. 'Officer. Me and my partner live with two other men. I can tell you their names. You can find them and they will clear this up'.

The sitting man noticed my change of posture and acted accordingly. 'Son, unless you can prove right now that these two men do in fact live at the same address, I'm afraid we will have to charge you with possession and intent to sell illegal drugs'.

I couldn't prove it on paper. Everything was in my name. Dallas and Pete had mentioned one time that they may not stay at the house much longer. We suggested the name and amenities go in my name so that Vicki and I could stay on when they leave. I thought nothing of it at the time. Who's to know that you'd have the cops knocking on your door one day and information like that would've been useful?

'I know. I'll call them. They'll straighten this up'.

The sitting man turned to look at Mr. pacing cop. Mr. pacing cop shoved his hand in his pocket and brought out a phone. It was my phone that they had confiscated back at the house.

I took it in my hands and went to Dallas' number. There was no answer. Not even a ring tome. It went straight to this message 'the number you are calling is not in service. Blah, blah, blah'.

'Doesn't sound like that number belongs to anyone'?

I stared at the sitting man. My heart beat fast and hard. My fingers fidgeted with the number pad. I didn't know a number for Pete.

Mr. pacing cop held his hand out, palm up, and gestured with his index finger for me to return the phone.

I did so.

'Looks like your *friend* isn't available?' Mr pacing cop always came in with the one-liners when he felt they were needed.

'You will be charged with possession and intent to sell Marijauna unless you can prove otherwise'.

Mr pacing cop again. 'And frankly, we'd have your girlfriend here too if it wasn't for the kid'.

'She's got nothing to do with this'.

'So you admit, again, that you are guilty?' Sitting guy was crafty and quick to pounce.

'I didn't say that'.

Man, Police have a way with words, mixing them and putting them into your mouth, don't they?

I decided to turn to the silent strategy from here on. Enough damage had been done.

When sitting man and Mr. pacing cop noticed this they took me back to my cell. They figured they had enough on me, and told me as much.

The next night, 28 hours and several more interrogations where I pleaded my innocence later, I was let out. I had a court date written on a summons shoved into my back pocket and a hell of a story to tell Vicki.

Mum was waiting for me in the holding area. She hugged me and led me to the car. I told her the whole story on the way home. She knew I had been into drugs so that was no surprise. She believed that I had given up for Joy. What she didn't believe was that I could live with such guys. And that I could let what they were doing go on while my Daughter was in the house.

It just occurred to me; I use to do drugs for Joy but then I gave up for the same reason. In name anyway. I don't know why I said that. Whatever gets you through the night I guess. (I love it when I unknowingly quote a classic Rock song).

It's all right.

By the time I was dropped off at home Mum had marked my court date in her mental calendar. She wouldn't let me do it alone.

When I walked into the house the hits kept coming.

I entered through the back door and was met with an empty room. There was no furniture anywhere.

I made my way down stairs where Vicki was feeding Joy. When she heard my steps Vicki put Joy down and met me with a hug.

'Oh god. What happened?'

'They think the drugs were ours. They said the only reason you weren't arrested as well was because of Joy'.

Vicki's face dropped. 'What? That's ludicrous'.

'You're telling me'.

I sat down on the couch next to where joy was sleeping. Taking her little hand in between my thumb and index finger I felt a sense of ease fall over me. That didn't last as I remembered the scene I had just walked through.

'Where's Dallas and Pete?'

'I don't know. I went to Mums place yesterday after all the stuff happened and when I came back the house was empty'.

'That's it? They haven't come back? You haven't heard from them?'

'Nope'.

'So what do you think happened?'

Vicki didn't have an answer. I told her the story about my time at the Station. She thought exactly the same as me.

'So someone told the cops that there were drugs in the house and it just so happened that we were the only ones home at the time that the Cops showed up?'

'I know. I was thinking the same thing.'

'So why would they do that?'

I found out why later.

Word got around, as it does, about my situation. Apparently Dallas and Pete had found out that the Police were watching our house due to high traffic coming and going. And as they both had prior convictions they didn't want another to deal with. It was probably around this time that they suggested they be removed from the lease and bills. I only have myself to blame for that. So Dallas and Pete waited for a day when they knew Vicki and I would be the only ones home and they made an anonymous call to the police. When I was at the Station and Vicki and Joy were at her Mums they returned and collected their stuff.

It took the heat off the both of them for the time being.

I was left to take the wrap for their crimes and I never saw either of them again.

Vicki and I took Joy and moved back into my Mum's place. We had three months of bliss and happy living before my court date arrived.

It was tight living. Suzie had moved into my old room since, besides Mum and Nathan's main bedroom, it was the biggest. I didn't mind this. There were too many bad memories in that room. I didn't want to have Joy anywhere near the room that I, apparently, learnt to be a man. This meant that Vicki, Joy and I had to cram into the smallest room in the house. When you consider that we all slept in one bed and had no other furniture, it wasn't all that bad.

The morning of my court date was uneventful. I woke up and had a shower like any other day. I sat down and had breakfast like any other morning. I brushed my teeth and fixed my hair like most other days. When I got dressed it was into one of Nathan's suits which, I don't need to tell you, was nothing like any other day.

Mum come along to the hearing. Vicki stayed home to watch Joy and was joined by Nathan and Suzie.

Suzie couldn't get enough of Joy. Any chance possible and she was holding my little daughter. Reading to her. Singing to her. Playing dolls with her.

They were more like sisters then Aunty and Niece.

Not a word was spoken by me or my Mum on the way to the court. She knew the situation I was in and the seriousness of it. But she also knew that I was innocent and was, not-willingly, taking the fall for it. The most nerving thing about it all was that Mum knew there was no out for me. I was most likely going to be found guilty and I was definitely going to have to pay.

What I don't think occurred to Mum yet was the fact that it hadn't even been three years since I was last in a courtroom. Remember, the Break and Enter drama with Scotty? I did community service at the Church of cheating wives.

When and if, no when . . . I was certain it would be when, this was pinned on me I would have another strike on my criminal record.

Criminal record? It hadn't occurred to me at the time that I even had a criminal record. I wasn't a criminal. Come on! I break into one house and get caught. Well, dobbed in by my friend but still. Now I am going to get in trouble for someone else's stash.

Life can be cruel.

Do you know what . . . ? I'm going to skip the whole court case drama. I'll sum it up for you real quick so we can move on.

This is a transcription from the hearing.

Judge: Did you live at the premises where the narcotics were found?

Me: Yes you honour, but I had two house mates.

Judge: Can you prove this? Were they on the lease?

Me: No.

Judge: So you were found in a house where there were drugs being sold?

Me: Yes but—

Judge: I find you guilty of possession with intent to sell illegal narcotics.

My Lawyer: Your honour, my client believes he was framed.

Judge: Can you prove it?

My Lawyer: No your honour. We can't find the men.

(Great Lawyer huh? I guess, that's what Government funding gets you.)

Judge: Decision is final. Fine stands at $2500 and you will serve 6 months in the ****** Correctional Facility.

Me/My Lawyer: Thank you your Honour.

Mum had tears in her eyes when I turned to face her. She embraced me and we walked out of the courthouse. The drive home was even more quiet then the trip to the court.

I had to tell Vicki the news when we got home. She broke down. Mum cried again. Suzie wasn't happy that they were both sad so she started crying. And because of all the noise Joy started screaming.

I would start my six month jail term in three weeks. I had to get in as much time with my loved ones as I could.

Because I lived back at home, I often ran into Scotty if he wasn't off with his new wench. When I told him about my conviction he said one thing—'Cool!'

Yeah right. It was fan-fucking-tastic!

Why did I persist on talking to this guy? Childhood friends . . . you can't shake them hey.

Those three weeks seem to be up in about two days.

It was *that* time.

CHAPTER 22
. . . .
Doing Time

Locked doors. Shared showers. No privacy. Lights out at 9. Barred-walls. The Yard. Standover Men. Shivs. Scared for my life. Falling asleep crying. Sexual advances from 6 foot 5, 120 kg men full of muscles, facial hair and confused fantasies. Missing Vicki. Not seeing Joy grow up.

These are the things I would have to get use to for the next 6 months of my life. There was no way around it. My life for the next 24 weeks would be spent behind bars, locked in a tiny, stinky, cramped, un-welcoming room with a stranger that may or may not try to make me his toy.

I would only be allowed to eat when and what I'm told. My lights would be turned off at 9pm exactly every single night and turned back on at 7am each morning. Not a second more or less. *Exactly!* My warden would tell me when I can go out into the yard to get exercise. He would, essentially, control when I would see the sun and feel its life-giving beams warming my paling skin. Mr. Warden would tell me when it was time to shower and I'm expected to be grateful to him for lumping me in there with the hardest criminals in the place. These guys didn't even wait for you to drop the soap. There didn't even have to be soap.

This was my pitiful existence for the next 6 months. Maybe less for good behaviour and trust me I was going to be the best they had ever seen.

My fellow inmates weren't helping my cause though.

My cellmate ordered me to not speak to him but whenever he addressed me I was to reply with 'Yes Smurf'. He was known all around the jail as Smurf. I won't tell you why he was called that. No, ok, I will. Why not. We all know what a Smurf is right? Those little blue creatures that only had one female to repopulate with a thousand male Smurfs. Busy girl. But the race survived so you have to give her credit for that, even if it meant she was a bit of a slut. Maybe that's why every guy fantasised about her growing up. I did. So that's the connection. Not the slut part. All though . . . No, the blue part. Smurf was queer and didn't try to hide it. Whether he was that way on the outside I don't know. That's irrelevant. I do know his name was Mac. Smurf would give any guy that asked a Blow Job for the right price. That was common knowledge. The first thing that came out of his mouth when we met was 'I'm Smurf. I'll suck your dick for a pack of sticks'. Sticks were cigarettes. I told him I wouldn't need his services, thank you. You would be asked almost every other minute for a cigarette by some burly inmate. If you were game enough to ask why they didn't have any, they would all reply the same. So a common term started going around the yard 'I just got blew by Mac'. So you had blew, which is like blue, the colour. So people started calling him Smurf because he blew everyone that had a spare

And luckily for me, I shared a room with him. I'd never seen so much action in my life. The man was on his knees more than the occupants of a Mosque. And, as you could imagine, our fellow jail birds thought I was in on the coup. I was offered so many packets of cigarettes I could've been a vending machine if I'd accepted them. I was assigned with a nickname. No one in jail is called by their real name. That's mainly because no one knew it and no one cared to find out. What was my nickname . . .

Smurfette.

Funny right? Sure, hilarious.

During my stay on the inside I would be known as Smurfette. It's funny how things catch on in the clink. My fellow innocent criminals (they're always innocent) knew that I didn't offer the same services but it didn't stop them from calling me Smurfette. It wasn't as easy to convince them that Smurf and I didn't spend our nights blowing each other. Hence the nicknames.

I tried to keep to myself on the inside but that's no easy task. Being the new guy in the block I was constantly heckled and tested. I was punched more time then a work card and knocked to the ground so much I could've been mistaken for a throw rug. Luckily it never went any further than that.

I think the old-timers in these places have been inside for so long that they have to get their fun, their kicks from wherever they can. That usually means scaring the hell out of young, fresh-faced new inmates. Just like me.

Your best bet as a newcomer is to take the brunt of all their jokes. Let them have their fun and push and punch you. Don't retaliate. With any luck a new target will come along and you'll be forgotten about.

I wasn't so lucky. For my 6 months in there I was always the new guy.

I don't know if I should be including this topic but I can't be picky right? If I'm going to tell my story I have to tell it all. The good, the bad and the ugly.

I can't just pick the happy, glorious moments and leave out all the shit that happened. That's what life is about right; Taking the good with the bad and having to live with them both.

Vicki couldn't bring herself to do that. She was all for the good times but when things got scary, serious, bad, she was nowhere to be seen. She never came by once to visit me while I was locked up. I can't blame her. I know it took Mum all her strength to visit me the few times that she did.

Our conversation was the same both times.

'How are you going love?'

'I'm ok.'

'Are you safe?'

'It's not too bad. How's Joy?'

'She's great love. Vicki too.'

'How about Suz?'

'She's doing good too. We all miss you love.'

'Yeah.'

Silence.

'Time's up', the guard would shout.

'Well I have to go. I'll see you next time'.

'Sure Mum. Kiss Joy for me'.

'Of course dear'.

I would sit at the table and chairs in the visitor's yard and watch Mum walk through into the holding area. From there I could see her pick up her bag and belongings and head on to the car park at the front of the jail.

I can honestly say that this was the only time I ever thought about hating my Mother. Watching her as she got to walk out of that place and back into freedom made me just a little bit spiteful. I hated her for being able to do that because I knew I was trapped and there was absolutely nothing I could do about it. That was the worst thing about being in jail—feeling helpless about your situation. No, I take that back. The worst thing, for me, about being in jail was *knowing* that I was innocent and shouldn't have been there.

I was four months into my sentence when my quiet existence within the walls was shattered.

Apparently Smurf had a run in with one of the big gang leaders. This was how it went . . .

Smurf had offered his service to this gang leader who had graciously accepted. I was in the room when it happened, trust me, he was gracious. All went well, for them, and the guy left feeling happy and relaxed. The only thing was that the gang leader didn't pay his fare. Smurf didn't dare shout out after the guy as it was lock down and it'd rouse the guards.

'Don't matter none'. Smurf mentioned 'I'll get them tomorrow'.

I don't know who he was talking to as I was pretending to be asleep.

The next day I was in the yard and watched as Smurf made his way over in the direction of the gang. The leader was sitting on the end of the weights bench lifting dumbbells in a curling fashion.

'What the fuck do you want, Smurf!?'

Smurf whimpered. 'Ah, you forgot to pay me'.

This sent the gang into an uproar. You see, as much as there were a lot of guys who utilised Smurfs talent, many of them never made it known.

They were billowing and hooting. The leader stood up like a dart and squared off against Smurf.

'The fuck are you talking about queer?!'

'Just. You—you didn't give me my packet'.

The gang were hollering and high-fiving each other. The funny thing about this was I bet at least half of them had given Smurf cartons of smokes.

The gang leader pouted his chest and poked Smurf with his finger.

'Get the fuck out of my face queer. Before I stab your fucking eyes out with my fork'.

Smurf stepped back, still being poked on the forehead. 'But, but—'.

'Fuck off now!'

The guards had noticed by this time and called for it to be broken up.

And here's where I came into it . . .

The gang leader had to explain himself to his broad. He explained it like this: 'That fucking Smurfette is spreading rumours. I want you to teach him a lesson'.

That night a small portion of the gang paid a visit to my cell. They were all familiar with the layout.

I copped the batteries-in-a-sock treatment. And you know what, they didn't even touch Smurf.

So I was in jail because of what someone else did, coping a beating because of what someone else did.

Such is life.

My six months came and went and one morning I found myself waiting out front in the car park for Mum to pick me up.

The car stopped directly in front of me. The boot opened so I could throw my bag in and I hopped in the front passenger seat.

'Thanks for getting me Mum'.

'No worries Darling'.

Mum drove away in silence

Jail hadn't taken my manners. That was a positive. It had skewered my thoughts though. It opened my eyes to life on the outside and how lucky we all were to have our freedom.

And it showed me how lucky I was to have a family.

Chapter 23

Family

Family is a rite of passage.

I never got that saying. What does it even mean? Webster's Dictionary defines 'Rite' as—*noun a ceremonial practice or procedure, esp religious*. While 'Passage' is, this is where it gets confusing—*noun act or right of passing*. Maybe that's what the saying is and I have it wrong? That'd explain why it makes no sense to me.

Family is a right of passing.

But then what does that mean? Does it mean that family is a passage? Because the Dictionary says that a Passage is a right of passing. It keeps going around in circles.

Confusing huh?

I'll leave it for someone else to figure out.

The reason I bring it up is because I want to take a moment to discuss family. I always thought it was lame whenever anyone said that all you need in life to be happy is a loving family. I would think "Surely not. What about endless mounds of money? A bevy of gorgeous women? A cool car?" All that materialistic stuff. Don't you need those things to be truly happy? Years ago, times mentioned in this story, I would've agreed with myself. But not now.

I am older, certainly not wiser but definitely smarter. I know that all of those other things don't matter if you don't have someone to share them with. The people in this world who are alone but have all those things don't realise this.

Case in point: Picture a wealthy 40 year old man. Let's say he's got his money by digging holes in the ground and producing black gunk. It doesn't matter how he got it. Let's assume he has. He's worked his whole life to attain riches that he couldn't spend in five lifetimes. The sacrifice made for his wealth is that he never took the time to start a family. Mind you, he can get any woman he wishes for a price and he drives the nicest car on the market. His house is so big that even he gets lost in it. Would you call this happy? I'm sure most of you probably said yes to yourself reading that last line. But I think you're wrong. When it's late at night, who has he got to go home to and talk about his day? Who has he got to wake up next to? He doesn't have anyone to share the nice car with. He has no one around to appreciate the nice things that money can buy. I bet when he sneezes in his big house it echoes throughout because it's that empty. Void of companionship. When the man hits 85 and starts having heart trouble whose there to tend to him? He's spent his whole life worrying about the next dollar, so much so that he's going to die with no one by his side. I don't call that a happy life.

Now picture this scenario: A struggling 40 year old man. He works 50 hours a week to put food on the table and a roof over the head of his family. He has a shit box of a car that barely gets him from A to B, but it does get him there. He rents a house in the suburbs because he'll never be able to afford to buy a house. But he has taken the time to start a family. He found his perfect partner and married her. Not long after they decided to have a child. Then another. Then maybe a third. Now he has a house full of love. Every night when he gets home from work he is hugged to death by a wife and three kids that adore their husband and father. They sit down every night around the kitchen table for dinner and conduct light banter about their days. After dinner they sit down and watch TV together, sharing laughs at the same time. There are goodnight kisses for all at bed time and then he gets into a warm bed next to his caring wife. In the morning he wakes up next to that same loving woman and his first thought is that he gets to do it all again. To him, this is the greatest feeling in the world. Now, do you think that this is happiness? I hope most of you just said yes, heck yes! I did. This man gets to share every good occasion, and bad, with a group of people that adore the very breath that he takes. When this man is 85 he has a hospital room full of children, grand-children and great grand-children by his side. That is his legacy. I would die a happy man if it were me. The happiest.

And what does it all come down to—Family.

You can tell, by previous topics that I didn't have the happiest childhood but my Mum always instilled into me the importance of family. She used to always say to me "I wish you a happy family and many years together". I think she said this because for the first 30 odd years of her life she didn't have it. She didn't want that fate to befall me.

I hope I've done her proud?

My family came into fruition later on in life. The day my real Dad showed up was like a catalyst (Webster's Dictionary page 63). It set things in motion. I think, without knowing—there's a term for that, let me grab the dictionary again—Subconsciously, that's it. Subconsciously I start understanding the importance of family. Dad never said anything particularly that triggered it. I think I saw how he conducted himself and the way he put family first, before anything and everything. He knew the importance of a family. I wonder who taught him? Did he learn from himself? Did his dad pass the knowledge down to him? Maybe that's the job of the Dad—pass on the importance of a family to his son so that he, in turn, can pass it on to his.

What if you only have Daughters? Does the same rule apply? Maybe the task is to pass it onto your children, regardless of gender.

Families are meant to be there for you right? No matter what. You could clearly be in the wrong but your family is still meant to support you because that's what they do. Families forgive, forget and move on. Am I wrong? Please, pull me up if I am. As I said, I was a late learner to these teachings. I don't need to remind you the lessons I was taught as a kid. Definitely not a family activity.

Should I say it? Do I really need to bring it up again? Ok, I will. Am I being naive for thinking such things? Like a lot of other things in my time, do I have families all wrong? No, I have to get something right.

Stop making me question myself. Bastards!

I know the importance of a family. My Dad told me so.

My family means everything to me. Mum. Dad. Suzie. Joy. Nathan. Carol. Every one of them. They all know how important they are to me. I hope. You do right?

So Vicki's name isn't mentioned in the list above? All will be revealed. Be patient.

Something that is just as important as family are friends. I don't mean just anyone that you may happen to know for a brief time in your life. I am referring to those people that stay in your life for a real long time. These are the people that see you for who and what you really are. Good or bad. I have only had a few in my time. Two of those were lost to time when I was 18. The third and probably last true friend I had was around a bit longer to see me grow up.

But not much.

CHAPTER 24

Death—Part 2

Nobody should ever have to experience losing a loved one. No matter what you've done in life you shouldn't have to deal with such a devastating time.

I had to go through the trauma when I was only 18 years old. Losing two of the best friends I will ever have is something I always have to accept and live with. Sometimes it's easy, sometimes not so much. You do actually forget about it for the most part. It isn't until you realise that you are not remembering your fallen friends that you feel guilty. You don't notice that you stop thinking about them. But I guess that's how you move on with your life right?

I have a regularly reoccurring dream where my friends haven't passed on. They've merely been away . . . for 15 years. In my dream I am sitting at home and Craig walks in as if nothing is wrong. 'Where have you been?' I say. 'Visiting family.' Just like that. He is back and never died. Then I wake up and feel guilty for not thinking about him in the past year.

I wonder if it is like this for every one?

I didn't have to wait long to see if it was easier the second time round.

Grace was a constant source of strength when I did my six month stint behind bars. She sent me a parcel of goodies every week. In it was a letter telling me how everyone was going at home. A new picture of Joy. A batch of freshly-baked cookies and, best of all, the latest edition of People magazine. I was surprised that all the contents made it to my cell as it had to be opened up and scanned by the guards. I was still able to turn every page of the mag though so that was a bonus (The same couldn't be said by the time I'd finished with it).

Once a month she would call me and we'd chat for my allocated 30 minutes. The conversation never went into me being where I was. She always spoke about the outside world and I always asked for more. I was never asked how I was going in there. For those 30 minutes each month Grace took my mind and spirit outside of those walls.

When I got out the first place I went to after home was to see Grace. She greeted me with open arms and a warm smile.

'Welcome home dear'.

'Thank you Grace'.

We were still hugging.

'Did I get the right magazines love?'

I let go. 'Sure. Thank you'.

'It was the least I could do. Tell me, how's your family going?'

I looked at her, smirking. 'You know very well how they're going. Mum tells me that you checked in on Joy most days. She has got a Mother you know'

'Sure dear. There's no harm in double-checking, is there? I was doing it for you son.'

'I know and I appreciate it.'

'It was my pleasure.'

I hugged her again. 'You're way too good to me Grace.'

'Nonsense dear.'

Grace helped me get back into a normal routine. I had Mum and Vicki at home to keep my feet grounded. Help me pick up where I left off. As best as I could anyway. Between both households I was slowly feeling like I belonged again. I know what you're thinking; it was only six months. That's not so bad. Oh yeah. You try it. No actually, don't. If you don't believe me, I don't mind. But do me, yourself and your family a favour and never find yourself having to test my judgement.

I had lost my job at the supermarket. They didn't hire criminals. Even if that supposed "criminal" had given them years of commitment prior to their false conviction, they couldn't have me on the payroll.

What Grace failed to mention during our monthly thirty-minute chat was that her health was rapidly deteriorating. She fell ill the week after I went inside and she had only got worse. Mum told me all about it on my first day back at home.

'She's not doing well dear'. I could sense the sorrow in Mum's voice. I think it wasn't so much that she was sorry Grace was ill (I know she was) it was the fact that I was about to go through something that nobody dealt with well. She felt sorry for me because she knew what was coming. She knew it was going to hit me . . . hard!

'How do you know?'

'I checked in on her every week while you . . . when you . . . because you . . .' Mum couldn't finish the sentence.

'Mum, its ok'.

How's that; everyone in my life was checking in on each other while I was doing my time. Grace was looking into the well being of my child and the mother of my child while Mum was doing the same for Grace. Who was looking after Mum? Maybe that was the gap left by my absence. She had Nathan I s'pose.

'And she was sick?'

'Well the first few times I went there she wasn't home. I found out from her *very* resourceful neighbour that she was frequenting the hospital. I hung around the next time I went there until she got home. We got to talking and she told me all about her health issues'.

'What's wrong with her?'

'She's just getting old love. Sometimes there's nothing necessarily wrong with a person. They just get old. The body stops working'.

'But how?'

'It just happens. I can only hope it happens to you'.

'What?! You hope I die?'

'No dear, I hope you live a long and happy life and eventually, when your time is up I hope you go peacefully and fulfilled. I'd rather that then having some terrible thing happen to you and you die from that at an early age'.

She had a point. 'Right. So what's wrong with Grace?'

'I just told you. She's an old woman. Her body is starting to tell her that it can't go on much longer'.

'Right'.

After this was revealed my visits to Grace doubled, tripled even, to the point that I spent more time there then at home. I started taking Joy over with me. That was my plan of attack. I was going to surround Grace with youth and life. I thought it might make her feel younger and, in turn, better. It turned out that, as much as you can feel young in the mind, your body will always bring you back to reality. Every visit stored the same conversation.

'How are you feeling Grace?'

Her answer was text book denial 'I'm doing wonderful'.

'What did the doctor say?'

Grace was required to go to the hospital every third day for monitoring. I would normally show up in between these visits.

'Oh they don't know'.

All old people think that doctors don't know what they're on about.

'Grace, they're doctors. They know what they're doing. Let them help you'.

'I'm ok love'.

The above transcription was never believable.

She was far from ok.

I asked everyone I knew what I should do. The responses were so similar that I couldn't help but take heed of them.

Vicki—'What can you do? She's old. We all have to die'.

Dad—'I think it is just her time son'.

Carol—'We all have to live with the knowledge that we're going to die eventually'.

Nathan—'She's had a good run. At this stage there's nothing you can do'.

Mum—'Love, all you can do is make the time she has left as pleasant and happy as you can and when the time comes, you just have to try to be strong'.

And that's what I did. Well half did. I did do my best to make her time as comfortable and happy as I possibly could. But I was anything but strong as the moment neared.

It was a cool Friday afternoon. I had just finished work. I got regular shift work at a local furniture manufacturing factory. I worked three days a week. Sometimes I got a few night shifts too. It was steady and I enjoyed it enough. I decided, instead of going home to shower, that I would head straight over to see Grace. I pulled up in the driveway, exited the car and started for the back door. As I rounded the side yard I heard the little radio she normally played when she sat down to read a book. Only, it was a lot louder than usual. I wondered how she could read and listen to the radio, even when it was low, at the same time and still concentrate on either, let alone both. There was no way she could do it at this volume. Besides, she was an old lady, they don't play loud music. Even if it is talk show chat hour. My concern heightened when I noticed spilt tea on the floor at the entry into the kitchen. There was a broken white china mug scattered amongst the tea.

'Grace?'

I knelt down and felt the tea. It was cold. The tea had been there for a while.

'Grace?'

I walked around the far side of the table and noticed a streak in the tea splashed on the floor. The cold liquid had been disturbed.

'Grace? Where are you?' My voice strained.

The disturbed tea stopped in the hallway where the linoleum met the carpet. There were a few streaks on the white carpet. When I turned the corner into the living room my small, insignificant life came crashing down around me. This was the beginning of my failed attempt at having the strength required to get through the situation.

At first you could've been forgiven for thinking there was a pile of unfolded blankets on the floor. But that was short lived when you noticed that the mattress cover had hair.

'Grace! Shit!'

I threw myself down beside Grace and rolled her over onto her back. Her eyes were open but they seemed distant.

'Grace, look at me.'

Her hair was messy, matted with tea that was also streaked down the front of her clothes. She had done her best to reach the telephone in the living room. Didn't quite make it. I would finish the job. I reached over from my position on the floor and picked the phone up. I dialled. After three rings it was answered.

'Hello?'

'Mum, its Grace! Something's wrong. She's on the floor'.

'Slow down love. What's she doing right now? Is she conscious?'

'Shit! Shit! She's lying on the floor in the lounge room'. I put my hand over her mouth and nose. 'She's not breathing. Shit! Shit!'

'Ok dear. Hang up and call an Ambulance. I'm on my way'.

'Ok'. I punched my finger on the latch and hit 000.

'What's the emergency please?'

'It's my friend. She's not breathing'.

15 minutes later the Ambulance arrived. My Mum had been at work on Grace for over 5 minutes by that time, to no avail. The Paramedics ushered Mum aside and crowded the lifeless body of Grace. They pumped her with those shock things that bring life back into people. They didn't work the first time. They were just as ineffective the third.

Mum held me close as Grace was wheeled into the ambulance. Not that you'd know it was her what with the big black zipper bag and all.

Four days later I found myself standing amongst a gathering of mostly strangers. This was one of the only times in my life that I fit in with my predominately all black outfit. I could've done without fitting in if this was the price. One of those people was Beth. I hadn't seen her since our affair had ended. I had no desire to see her. Not even now. *Especially* not now. I said my hello's to everyone I knew and politely asked to be excused. I wanted to be alone.

The service was held inside. Grace had requested she be cremated. Her family granted that wish. I was seated in the front row the whole time wondering how I had got there. A little old lady whose purse I once stole had become one of my greatest friends. And now she was gone.

In four years I had lost my two best friends in one swift swoop, I got sent to Jail for a crime I didn't commit and now one of the greatest, loveliest, kindest, happiest, friendliest people I had ever had the privilege of knowing was taken away from me.

The world hadn't done me any favours.

I didn't know why I'd deserved it.

CHAPTER 25

. . . .

Hindsight

What a wonderful concept—Hindsight. Just the idea that you could know, beforehand, what you were going to do and, if you so desired, prevent yourself from doing it. Seems too good to be true doesn't it? I guess that's why it doesn't exist. We all wish we had it though.

If you could give me a moment to push my point . . .

I bet Pete Best wishes he had the hindsight to see how huge that little band he was in would go on to become after he left. Imagine; August 12th 1962. You are asked to join a band that is set to head off on a trip to Hamburg to play dingy, crowded clubs. You're set at a drum kit behind three guys in black leather pants and jackets with jersey boy haircuts playing their hearts out on their selected instrument—Guitars. You are covering hits by all the big names of yesterday. Everything's perfect, in your eyes at least. You are travelling around the world meeting pretty girls and having a blast of a time.

Two years, and many Hamburg trips, later you are asked to leave the band with no explanation. From that day on you will forever be referred to as "The Fifth Beatle".

And what does the rest of the band do? They find a replacement Drummer with a weird name, write a little pop ditty called 'Love Me Do' and go on to become, without contest, the greatest band the world has ever seen.

And what, I hear you ask, became of Pete Best—for the next 20 years of his life he became a Civil Servant. He did eventually get back into music. He started his own band called The Pete Best Group. (At least you can't get fired from a band with your name in it). And did they go on to heights anywhere near that of The Beatles? Let me ask you this: Have you ever heard of The Pete best Group?

If Pete had his time over again, knowing what he does know, I guarantee you that the world would never have heard of Ringo Starr.

Let's look at JFK. John F Kennedy. The 35th President of the USA. It happened on what was a warm, sunny day in Dallas, Texas. The 22nd November 1963 was forecast as a cooler day. If that had been the case the car John and his wife, Jacqui were riding in may have had the roof closed. Instead, at 12:30pm they made their way through the city streets with the roof of their convertible down. At the tender young age of 46 he was shot through the head and died on the scene. He slumped into the lap of his wife sitting beside him with his skull peeling away from his head. Could you imagine that?

The crime was pinned on a chap by the name of Lee Harvey Oswald who was shot two days later, while in Police custody, before any trial was set (Would

Lee have benefited from Hindsight? Would he have changed anything?). The man who shot Lee Harvey was Jack Ruby. Jack was convicted of murdering the man who assassinated John F. Kennedy. Is that justice for JFK's death?

The sad part is that JFK had served in World War 2. He was a part of the Solomon Islands Campaign. The man managed to survive the bloodiest, most taxing War man has ever seen, but a lunch time drive through the streets of Dallas . . . that he couldn't get through.

If JFK had hindsight at his disposal I am certain he would've put the roof up on his convertible. Better yet, he wouldn't have been in the car or in the State for that matter.

If Lee Harvey and Jack Ruby had hindsight I think they wouldn't have changed anything. I mean, their names are recorded in history now. Would you want to change that? Regardless of the circumstance surrounding it?

How about the Fuhrer—Adolf Hitler. This guy survived in World War 1. A primitive war that claimed so many lives and Adolf made it through. What're the odds? He was even captured by the Allied Forces and later released. This opened his eyes to the possibilities before him. He wasted no time in making a name for himself. He went straight into Politics. (War is politics right?). Challenging all who opposed him, he pushed to become leader of the Nazi party.

(Most people think Hitler invented what the world now knows as the Nazi's. But this is very wrong. The Nazi's were a political party long before Hitler got involved. Hitler merely brought them up through the ranks, lifted them to prominence and slightly sent their beliefs and actions askew. But the term "Nazi" was already in existence).

In 1938, 20 years since Hitler survived WWI, he had gained the power that he so sought and thought he deserved. The first important item on his agenda was to unify all German-speaking people. He annexed Austria then demanded the liberation of German people in the Sudetenland region of Czechoslovakia.

One year later, 1939, he had occupied Czech and set about invading Poland. It was at this time that England and France declared war on Adolf Hitler and the entire nation of Germany, and their main allies—Italy. This was the official start of what would become World War 2.

Within another year, 1940, whilst fending off the Brits and France on one front, Hitler invaded and occupied Denmark and Norway to safeguard supply routes of Swedish ore and also to establish a Norwegian base from which to break the British naval blockade on Germany. Hitler launched his "Blitzkrieg" (lighting war) against Holland and Belgium. Rotterdam were bombed almost to extinction. Both countries were occupied.

It was not long after this that Japan, working on Germany's side attacked USA, converting Pearl Harbour into a cemetery. This forced America to wake up the sleeping beast that it was and join in the battle to stop this tyrant.

Now if we fast track many years, and millions of dead people later, Hitler is dead in his bunker with his new wife Eva Braun by his side. Both with a bullet in the head of their smouldering corpses.

So I pose this to you; If Hitler had hindsight what would he change knowing that the end result was the death of him himself and his wife? Would he not have run for Parliament which lead to the whole fiasco in the first place? Once he had that power there was no way that he wasn't going to use it. Could he have got to power but decided to never have overthrown the Czechs or Polish? He could've been content with being the leader of an economically thriving country. (All thought the only reason they were thriving was because of Adolf and his war effort). Or, and most unlikely, would he have had the hindsight to know when he was defeated and put a stop to the senseless murder of millions of soldiers and innocent civilians?

One thing's for sure, if he had stopped any of those events the world may be a different place. But if he succeeded it would've certainly been for the worse.

Maybe we'll leave hindsight out of it in Adolf Hitler's case. If you don't mind?

Now that I think about it, it may have been better for the Allieds to have hindsight. If they did, they would've hunted and killed the bastard during the First World War. Then there never would've been a second.

These are just thought I have. Sometimes that's all there is to do here.

I don't know why I'm devoting so much time to hindsight. I may have mentioned it once, in passing, throughout the whole story and now I can't stop talking about it. I think I'm procrastinating. Putting off going on any further because I am looking at my list of topics that I started with and I am not too keen on the next one at all.

I guess. Let's get it out of the way.

Here's goes nothing.

Strike 3 . . . You're out of here!

CHAPTER 26

Strike 3

After Grace's death I began to have a different attitude toward life. My character was becoming a little askew. In years previous I may have had a more positive, upbeat attitude but after the passing of another great friend I started finding the negatives in most situations.

Maybe the change started before Grace's death. Is it possible that my six month stint in jail had affected me more than I thought? I said earlier that it hadn't taken my manners but it may have altered my conception. It might have opened my eyes to the bad in the world. Can it be as simple as that to change who you are? I saw some bad things when I was inside. And barely escaped many more. That has to change a person, right?

Maybe that's why I found myself spending more time with Scotty again.

Isn't it funny how people come in and out of your life? I didn't see any of the guys I grew up with anymore. They'd all grown up and got married, started a family, went away to work or just disappeared. Maybe if we had all stuck together my life could have turned out different. No use pondering on what could have been. What happens happens and there's no changing it. It's not fate or destiny, its life.

When I think about it, I was one of the guys that went off and did my own thing. Did I leave my friends or vice-versa?

But a few bouts of bad luck had tarnished my plan of settling down. Did I have a plan? It just happened. I moved out of home with Vicki. Left my old life and friends behind and looked ahead. I had a beautiful Daughter that I'd do anything for. I had responsibilities now. I was the man that had to put food on the table, clothes on their backs and a roof over their head. So the roof part landed me in trouble. You couldn't have guessed that that'd happen. (Should I refer back to Hindsight?)

Your life is like a revolving door. People leave and come back. They leave again and sometimes return. Most of the time it happens without you even noticing. I bet there's not a lot of people out there that can say they're still in touch with friends they had in primary school. High School even.

But I had come full circle. Back to where I was as a 9 year old boy. Living next door to this kid that has forever been a bad influence on me but I had always found myself drawn to.

I had moved back into Mum's place with Vicki and Joy and more often than not Scotty was over. He was clearly becoming a staple in my life again. And do you know what—he thought it was great that I had been behind bars. He was forever asking me questions about it.

'What was it like in there?'

'Bad'.

'What kind of stuff did you see?'

'Bad'.

'What was your cell mate like?'

'Bad'.

'Come on, tell me some stories'.

'Why do you want to know about it?'

'I want to know what it's like in jail'.

'Why?'

'I think it'd be cool. It'd toughen you up. You'd come out a bad-arse motherfucker'.

Is that who I was meant to be?

'Am I?'

'Don't know. Are you?'

'Don't think so'.

Mum and Vicki would tell you that I was far from it. I still was how I had always been—a quiet, polite, everyday guy. I would use my please's and thank you's. I'd hold the door for a female and give up my seat on the bus for the elderly. I'd give my last dollar to a friend in need and would do anything for my family. From the outside I was still the same old me. But on the inside—the deep, dark alleys of my mind, I would have different thoughts. I couldn't tell you where they stemmed from. I can tell you that it wasn't all from spending time in jail. I think it just happens that after enough bad luck in your time you start believing it's the only kind. Then before you know it you start conforming to it.

I'm not trying to make excuses I'm just preparing you for what's coming next.

It was a normal day like any other. Almost. I was at work earning my meagre wage while Vicki was at home tending to Joy. 5 o'clock came and I clocked off. The only difference with this particular Friday was that normally I would stop on the way home to pick up a six pack of beer. For some reason I didn't do that this time. I made the decision to head straight home and see Joy and Vicki. I pulled into the driveway and from the outside everything looked normal. Mum's car wasn't there. She was doing the late shift at the Chemist. Nathan was with Suzie at dance practice. I expected to walk in to be greeted by Vicki, with Joy in her arms. That's what I lived for. Walking up the front stairs the silence that hit me was deafening. I knew something wasn't right. Vicki and Joy were nowhere to be seen. I called a few times but there was no reply.

'Vicki? Vick?' Nothing.

Then I heard laughter and music. It was coming from the room Vicki and I shared. I started down the hall and the closer I got to the closed door the louder the laughter got. It started over-powering the music. I stopped at the doorway for a moment (I'm still not sure why I hesitated) before I turned the handle.

This was that split second moment, with the decision to go with it that changes your life forever. The swinging open of the door was also the closing shut of all faith I had in the human race. A metaphor I guess you could say.

Scotty was sitting on the bed with his legs dangling over the side. He had nothing but a pair of boxes shorts on, laughing at seemingly nothing. Vicki was sitting down on the floor, leaning against the bed. She was virtually in between Scotty's legs. It wasn't their attire (or lack of) or positioning that caught my attention, it was what Vicki had to her lips when I entered the room. One of her hands held a lighter. The other hand was holding an all too familiar device to her mouth. She was sucking for all her life on a Poor man's bong.

Scotty stopped laughing when he noticed me standing in the doorway. 'Hey man. How's it going?'

I looked at him but didn't respond. My attention turned to Vicki. She finished sucking on the bong, held the smoke in and eventually exhaled. 'Shit'.

That was all she could say—shit!

'What's going on?' I hadn't moved from the doorway.

Scotty took the bong from Vicki and packed the cone. 'Wanna hit?'

I couldn't believe the cool and calm of this guy—my apparent friend. I assumed by the way they were dressed and the manner of their positioning that they had been doing more than smoking pot. I looked at the bed to see if there was crumpled up sheets and discarded clothes but I found more then I bargained for.

My heart rate sky-rocketed. 'What the fuck is she doing in here?'

Vicki looked at Joy asleep on the bed then to me. 'I had to keep an eye on her'.

'So you put her in a room where there's smoke everywhere?!'

'I had nowhere else to put her'.

'Dude, she's asleep. She can't smell it'.

Yep, Scotty was that stupid.

'Who the fuck was talking to you?'

Vicki was visibly becoming sheepish and defensive. 'She's ok. Why are you home already?'

'Don't change the subject. What's going on here? Why do you have a bong to your mouth and why do you have my daughter in the same room? And where the *fuck* are your clothes?'

I had, up until this moment, only ever had one fight in my life. I went 20 odd years with only ever having to raise a fist against one other person and that was the man who posed as my Dad when I was a child. I don't count the confrontations I had in jail as fights because they were one-sided and cowering in a corner doesn't count. But that all changed when Scotty replied.

'Man, I think we left her clothes in your Mum's room'.

'Shut up Scott!' Vicki's shout woke Joy. She blamed it on me. 'Now look what you've done. I just got her down again'.

'Looks like she's not the only one that went down'. I couldn't help myself.

Scotty laughed at this. Was I that bad when I was addicted to drugs—Laughing at stupid shit that was far from funny?

He stopped laughing when I launched myself at him, jumping right over Vicki as she tended to the screaming baby.

'Whoa. Woah. Hey man—'

Vicki was shouting over Joy's crying 'Stop it! You're scaring her!'

I was on auto pilot and my setting was stuck on destroy. I swung a quick left and caught Scotty on the chin, ignoring Vicki as I surged. When Scotty started staggering I wrapped both of my hands around his neck and squeezed. As he struggled I looked over to where Vicki was picking Joy up. Once she had my daughter in her arms Vicki ran straight for the door. I was concentrating too much on Vicki and Joy, I must've been, because Scotty had managed to get one of my hands cleared from his windpipe and before I knew it he had landed a punch square into my stomach. Vicki and Joy were heard shouting and crying from the lounge room. With Scotty free from my grasp he had managed to regain his footing and was shaping up to me. I didn't care to go toe to toe with him. I lowered my shoulder and charged at the enemy. I caught him under the rib cage and we crashed into the far wall. The cupboard leaning against the wall was dislodged, drawers landed on the floor in a heap. Scotty pushed me back in resistance and we trampled the drawers. Wood panelling from the drawers crushed and splintered under the weight of our scurrying feet. We both veered sideways into a free standing mirror, knocking it over. Glass shards were sent pummelling to the ground. Now we were standing over dismantled drawers and shattered glass, locked together in a wrestlers embrace.

Joy was still screaming but I managed to hear Vicki's voice over the top of it. 'Please hurry. Someone's going to get hurt'.

Scotty pushed me back. I retaliated by using all my might to force him back toward the wall with the cupboard. Scotty lost his footing, fell back and crashed to the floor. I lost my grip on him during the fall. On his descent to the floor, Scotty whacked his head on the side of the cupboard that had managed to stay in place against the wall. There was no movement whatsoever when he slumped to the floor. Vicki ran in, stopped at the doorway, looked over to where Scotty laid, blood pouring from his head, and screamed some more.

'I'm—I—We were-'. I was struck for words.

'What happened?'

'He fell and hit his head'.

'Is he breathing?'

I walked over and stood above Scotty's still body, cracking glass and wood with each step. I leant down and put my finger to his throat. My hand marks were still visible from earlier. I had never had to feel for a pulse before but I'd seen it done in movies. There was no pulse.

'No'.

Fuck!

'What did you do?'

'What do you mean what did I do? What the fuck were you two doing?'

'Now's not the time?'

I stood and looked down at Scotty's pulse-free corpse. I heard sirens in the distance. 'What did you do?'

Vicki backed slowly out of the doorway. She turned and ran down the hall toward the front door. I followed leaving Scotty where he laid, still motionless.

I heard the sirens get louder and then saw them rounding the corner. Two Police cars pulled into the driveway as I went out onto the front porch. Vicki was in the yard waving her arms in the direction of the blue and white cars. Two Police Officers jumped out of each car and started for the gate where Vicki met them. I stopped dead in my tracks at the bottom of the stairs. I froze. Three Police men and one woman were slowly encroaching on my position at the stair base. They had one hand resting on the butt of their guns. They had previously unclipped the holster.

'There's someone upstairs. He's not breathing'. Vicki was speaking in gasps.

One of the Police Officers signalled for two of the others to head into the house. They walked past, eyeing me suspiciously and went up the stairs. The two remaining Officers kept their distance from me and their hands rested on their piece.

Vicki shouted orders from her place beside the Police.

'He killed the guy in there. He's dangerous'.

This comment was confirmed by way of the two-way radio perched on one of the Officers shoulder.

"We have an unconscious man in the back room. No sign of breathing. Large laceration on the side of his head. Ambulance required'.

The Officer with the talking shoulder replied. 'Copy that. Calling for Medical support'. He started for the car but not before looking at his partner, pointing at me. 'Detain him'.

In the blink of an eye I was handcuffed and being led to the squad car. Vicki was standing off to the side crying. I couldn't look at her. And with the most perfect of timing Mum, Nathan and Suzie all pulled up outside the yard. Mum exited her car in a hurry and went straight up to Vicki. She had not noticed me sitting in the back of the car.

'Vicki, what's going on?'

Vicki said nothing and pointed in my direction. Mum's mouth gaped open when she noticed me sitting in the rear of the car. She run up to the door but couldn't open it. She tapped on the window, I don't know why.

Pleading for me to be let out, Mum started crying and had to be removed from the car by one of the other Officers.

'Mrs. Please, you have to move away. If you follow us to the station we can sort everything out there'.

Nathan had to help contain Mum. Suzie was crying, holding onto Mum's side. The three of them embraced and sobbed.

As the Police car I was riding in pulled away from the street an Ambulance took its place. The last sight I saw before we turned the corner was of Mum collapsing onto the ground and Nathan following to console her. Suzie stayed where she stood, crying more.

I like to think I was a person with self control. I would call myself Stoic. As much as bad luck had its way of finding me, I think I generally kept myself under control. I was tragic but I was contained. I guess you could say I was a tragic with self control.

But there's one place where you have no choice but to give up that control. Maybe not so much give it up as have it taken from you.

CHAPTER 27

From the Inside

It feels like God and the Devil played a hand for my life and I lost. I don't know who was representing me.

No no, that can't be. I don't believe in all that Hocus Pocus.

I lived my life so I'm to blame. And I don't want any of you thinking any different.

Have you ever felt like no matter how much you try to do good, no matter how positive you wanted to be, you couldn't help but win the short straw and have it all turn to shit? That's been my life in a nutshell. I tried virtually all of my live to life well, happy and right. I followed rules and helped where I could. Yet here I am—34 years old and into the 10th year of a life term sentence for killing my neighbour.

So now you can tell me. Did you know it was going to end here? This unholiest of unholy places. Did you have an inkling, even the slightest, that I was writing my story from the comfortable confines of my 4 by 4 cell? I tried not to make it known while I took you through the story that has been my life that I was writing it from Prison. I don't know why I kept it from you. Maybe I didn't want it to sway your judgement of me. It means a lot to me if I am judged by the good that I have done in life. Not by the very rare mistake or misjudgement that has got me to where I am today.

Let me take this opportunity to give you the full story of how I came to be . . . well . . . you know where I am now. I'm not repeating it.

You already know the part about Scotty and me fighting. And you know that that ended with me being carted away in the back of a Police car. At the same time Scotty's lifeless body was being transported to the Hospital in the back of an Ambulance. He was pronounced dead at the scene. The knock he took to the head when he lost his footing is what did it. It caused internal haemorrhaging around the skull and killed him instantly.

Now obviously it was an accident and if I could go back in time I'd change it but what's done is done. I can never reverse the fact that I killed a man with my own hands. A friend for that matter. I mean, no matter how much of a bad influence he was on me through most of my life and regardless of the amount of times he may have pissed me off and I felt like killing him (Sorry, bad choice of words) he was still a friend.

But what kind of friend sleeps with your girlfriend? The mother of your child. That fateful day that I took his life, I had barely missed the latest fuckfest that Scotty and Vicki were frequently engaging in. It had been going on since not long after we moved back into Mums. During my trial I asked Vicki "Why?" Her answer "Because he was there". How do you like that? Sounds like someone else in my tales right? Beth. Ring a bell?

I know what you're thinking right now—I'm a hypocrite. I had an 18 month affair with a married, church-going girl. (I should stop referring to her as church-going, as if that'd stop her from doing what she did/does. It wouldn't. Church and Religion is a facade. That's just my opinion. Deal with it). But it's different when it happens to you. Isn't it?

Scotty had also got Vicki hooked back on Marijuana. Miss "you have to quit smoking pot because I'm pregnant and can't do it" had gone back to her old vice. She was getting high with Scotty everyday while I was at work. They'd get high as all shit and fuck. That use to be our thing.

Maybe Scotty deserved what he got?

And how did my family fair? How'd they take to my new lifestyle?

Mum was devastated. As would be imagined. During my whole trial she pleaded my innocence. 'My son is not a murderer' she would cry out to the jury. She kept whispering into my Solicitors ear 'Don't they know it was an accident?' The judge was all too aware that it was an accident but I was still sentenced to 25 years for involuntary manslaughter. I can get out in 15 with real good behaviour. It's really hard to behaviour in Prison though. You become a victim of circumstance. Your environment affects your psyche. There's no avoiding it. Mum could never, and still can't, live with the fact that her only son is in jail for manslaughter. Even if it is involuntary.

Thanks for being you Mum.

Nathan had to be Mum's rock. He and I had grown close over the years. He was my Step Dad after all. I don't really have much to say about Nathan. He is there for my Mum and that's all I need to know. And Suzie. Suzie calls him Dad and worships the ground he walks.

Little Suzie barely understood what happened at the time. When she celebrated her 10th birthday, my 2nd anniversary on the inside, Mum sent me a picture of her blowing out the candles on her cake. Mum kept her away from the courts the whole time my trial was happening. Scotty's Mum looked after her. The irony—This lady was willing to babysit the little sister of the guy that killed her only son. She really was as beautiful inside as she was out. When her friends ask her where her big brother has gone, Suzie automated response is 'He doesn't live at home anymore'. That's it.

Now that she's older, gee she'd be 18 now, Suzie is well aware of why I'm here. She writes me every month.

You'll always be my Little Suzie.

Dad and Carol were there throughout my entire trial. Dad had actually recommended, hired and paid for my Solicitor. It was a man that Dad served with in the Vietnam War. The guy was a hard-arse. A real leatherneck as they say. Dad insisted that if anyone could get me off it would be his friend the Solicitor. We can't win them all Dad. Every time Dad comes to visit me he apologises for me being where I am. It's ok Dad. It's not your friend the Solicitor that landed me in here; it was me and my moment of stupidity. And that Bad luck I seemed to have carried with me throughout my existence.

Can I pass on a piece of advice to anyone out there that is willing to listen? If you don't know your Dad, or have had a fall out with him, or merely lost touch, do yourself a huge favour and rekindle that relationship. Or go out and find him. One of the best decisions I ever made was to let my Dad into my life. He made it richer. My Dad is the greatest man I know. He lives a simple, humble life. He immerses himself with family and friends. He enjoys life and everything it has to offer.

Keep Rocking Dad. You're an inspiration.

Vicki. I'm not even going to acknowledge you, Vicki. You did one good thing in your life and that was to give birth to my beautiful daughter Joy.

Joy. She has no idea who her Dad is. I mean she knows me, she knows that I am her Dad but she doesn't know *who* I am. And I have no idea if I want it to be kept like that or not.

What would you do? Maybe I should get a survey going in here—

"Would you want your 10 year old (God, time flies!) Daughter to know the real you and why you are where you are?"

The results were no surprise.

24 said no.

8 said yes.

368 said Fuck Off!

Maybe they were the wrong demographic to ask. Maybe If I had asked them the amount of stash they're ladies were bringing them during the next visit hours I may have had a more positive response.

Ah well.

Visiting Hours. Gee, that gets me thinking. They take on a whole new meaning now which I could go into but it's almost time and they'll be first through the gate. Mum brings her nowadays. Apparently Vicki can't bring herself to visit. I wonder why. Funny, I don't remember asking her to.

My little Joy is always so happy to see her Daddy. She squeezes me harder than you do a pillow on a cold, rainy morning. I have to be grateful for that. I've asked Mum and Vicki to never tell her why I'm here. And she never cares to ask.

It doesn't matter to her.

Kids . . . so innocent in thinking that we're all so innocent.

Today's the day I give Joy this project that I've spent the last ten years working on. I know she won't be able to read it for a while, but that may be the point. Maybe I'd rather her not.

Anyway, she can read it when she's old enough. Judge me for herself.

I know what you're saying. I bet if it were you writing about your life you'd tell heaps of lies to make it more interesting. I can imagine you saying "If I tell my story I'm going to exaggerate the shit out of it! But I tell you, the truth is always better.

And besides, this isn't your life story, it's mine. The story of . . . wait . . . I just realised something. I never told you my name throughout this whole journey. Maybe it was a conscious decision from the get go. I think that stems from the fact that I have rarely been called by my name since I stepped foot inside this hell on earth.

How about if you just call me Prisoner number 120989.

I will say this—It's been a releasing experience writing my life story down on paper. Who knew I could fill so many pages?

It's funny. I improved my Grammar by sitting down, hiring out a Dictionary and writing about my life. I hope the improvement was noticeable. I did stop telling you what pages of the Dictionary I found the hard words on.

And I guess, I now know what the word Grammar means so I must've done ok.

And you'll never believe it but I have actually started loaning books other then the dictionary from our little library. On my library card (that's right, we even have library cards in prison) it states that I've borrowed the dictionary a total of 32 times. At 3 months a stint that means I have had it in my possession for 8 years. 8 bloody years! I *should* be well versed in grammar by now. I guess it's some other guys turn to tell their story.

And what have I hired the other two years I have been in here? A couple of times I didn't hire anything at all. When I had a lull in writing I didn't need the dictionary and didn't feel like venturing out to track down books I may like to try to read. The other times I did fell like tracking down some authors I didn't know where to start. I looked for any book in our library that was old and had the word "classic" written anywhere on the cover. There were a few. I have read some J.D. Salinger. Fyodor Dostoevsky. Cormack McCarthy. H.G. Wells. I hired war and Peace once, when I was feeling ambitious. I never got through it. Maybe it's time to finish that book.

I have become a fan of reading. I wouldn't call myself a "Bookworm". I'd probably fall into the "Book slug" category. I will read a book but will have to borrow it twice in a row to do so. Maybe more sometimes.

I guess my love of reading stemmed from me writing my story. It taught me to appreciate the value, and power of words. Is that irony? Shit, don't tell me I need the Dictionary?

I quite enjoy writing. One day I may even try to write a book.

I'm probably just naive enough to think that I could.

CHAPTER 28

Starting Over